KYLE, JACK, & RYAN

DEVIL SOULS MC NOVELLAS

LEANN ASHERS

COPYRIGHT

Kyle, Jackson, Ryan is a work of fiction. Names, characters, places, and incidents are all products of the author's imagination and are used fictitiously. Any resemblance to actual events, locales, or persons, living or dead, is entirely coincidental.

Except as permitted under the US Copyright Act of 1976, no part of this publication may be reproduced, distributed, or transmitted in any form, by any means, or stored in a database or retrieval system without the prior written permission of the author.

Designer: Regina Wamba

Photographer: Wander Aquilar

Editor: Aquila Editing

Formatter: HJ bellus

KYLE

1

CHRYSTAL

I CLENCH MY EYES CLOSED, wanting to go back to the dreams because my reality at the moment is shitty.

Cool air seeps into the vehicle, bringing me further and further out of my sleep, and my back is absolutely killing me. I have been sleeping in my car for the past three months. I drove and drove until I ended up in the small town of Raleigh, Texas just a few weeks ago.

I sit up and rub my eyes, dragging the blanket up to my neck, trying to conserve what body heat I can. Fog is covering the windows, but I can see the sun barely peeking out over the mountains.

I need to settle down and find a place to stay for a while. I feel my baby kick inside me. I smile, running my hand over my stomach. I'm pregnant, five months to be exact. I found out when I was eight weeks along, and ever since I have been on the run.

I'm working in a garage at the moment, as a receptionist. I'll stay here in my vehicle until I have a down payment for an apartment—I spent all my savings on gas and gas station food—then I'll start to get settled.

I'm sleeping in the back of the garage; it's chained, which makes me feel safer. I have keys to the building, so I can sneak inside and shower and use the kitchen. At least I can warm up in the shower if it gets really cold outside.

It's honestly heaven compared to what I've been used to. Heck, I've slept on the floor in front of my desk. The one thing that does worry me is that they don't know I'm sleeping back here. But I am safe; that's what matters most to me at the moment.

I am twenty-two years old, and I'm in this situation because I left my husband.

I started dating him when I was just sixteen. My mom kind of set it up because we lived in a trailer in the middle of nowhere and this guy was rich. I was her ticket out.

I didn't want that. I wanted to be independent and go to college. I wanted to make a life for myself. And, at twenty-eight years old, he was way too old for me. But I didn't want to disappoint my family.

So I married him two weeks after I graduated from high school. All my friends were living their best life and partying, and I was buying decorations for my wedding.

This was essentially an arranged marriage. The day of the wedding, I walked down the aisle with tears in my eyes because I was so miserable, but I had to plaster on a fake smile. My mother cried in the front pew, in her new dress that my husband had bought for her. He gave her a credit card, and she's now living in a new apartment with new clothes and a new life. All she had to do was give him me. My dad has tried to be happy for me, he's tried to be there for me, but my mother is completely impossible.

I said my "I do," and he took me to our new house, where I had sex for the first time. It was not horrible, but I didn't enjoy one single second of it. The first few years of our marriage were bad, but it was nothing compared to the last year. That's when his temper came out. It started when I accidentally spilled his plate of food in his lap as I brought it to the table. The next thing I knew, a fist was planted into my face.

In that single moment, my world changed. I went to my mom with the full intention of leaving him, because I couldn't stay with a man who was abusive. That was not me.

My mother all but slammed the door in my face and told me that I needed to be better at serving my husband. It was my job to take care of him and I pretty much deserved what he had done to me.

I realized in that very moment I was so alone. I felt sad, but I was not defeated. I hatched a plan to get out, but I couldn't just run with nothing. So I suffered. He beat me, hurt me, and broke me every single day. That one punch to my face changed my life.

So it took a whole year. I had to buy a vehicle that was not in his name, and I had to have money to live on for as long as possible. But then I found out I was pregnant, so I had the urge to leave that second. Hurting me was one thing, but allowing my unborn child to be hurt was unthinkable.

He left on a business trip for a week, and he never called when he was gone, so I took that as my time to go. I knew the second he was home he would call me, so I threw out my phone immediately. I had no one that wanted to talk to me anyway.

I open my car door and sneak inside the garage so I can shower and get ready for the day. The second I step inside, the heat hits me and it takes everything I have not to moan. You never fully realize how much the small things mean until you don't have them anymore. Just to be able to wake up in a warm place would be amazing. I know I'll never take anything for granted again.

I hurry to shower and get dressed before all the guys show up. I was kind of worried because this business belongs to the

Devil Souls MC, but my coworkers are all really nice. I put on a pot of coffee for the guys and settle back in my seat, rubbing my belly and smiling. "I can't wait to meet you."

I will not fail her. I will not fail her like my parents did me. I will protect her from anything that would dare to harm her.

"Good morning, darlin'."

I jump in my seat, not having expected that beautiful voice. I look up at the hottest man I have ever laid eyes on in my life. I swallow hard, my mouth dry. I haven't seen him before. I eye his cut and see the tag on the front. He's the president of the Devil Souls MC.

I heard that he was coming in today, but I never expected him to look like that. I wipe my hand on the front of my jeans and start to stand up, but he shakes his head. "I brought you breakfast." He sets a bag on the counter in front of me and pulls up a seat on the other side of my desk so he's facing me.

He hands me a small take-out plate and then sets one in front of himself. What is going on?

Kyle

I can see the shock on her face as I put the food in front of her. She doesn't know that we know she's staying in the garage, but we knew from the cameras the second she pulled her vehicle around to the back the first day she got off work.

I've been out of town for a month, working on businesses we have in surrounding counties.

I decided today to get on her fucking good side by bringing food, so I can move her out of the car into an apartment or something, but I never expected her to be absolutely fucking drop-dead gorgeous. I almost ate my tongue at the sight of her holding her stomach with an angelic smile on her face. Her eyes are the bluest I have ever seen in my life, and her blond hair has a slight wave to it, begging for me to dig my hands in.

She tilts her head, studying me as I'm studying her; then she slowly opens the breakfast I brought from the diner. "Thank you for breakfast." I want to close my eyes like a fucking pussy, because her voice is heaven. The dark always craves the light, and right now it's wanting her. I smirk. "You're welcome, darlin'."

She blushes and pours syrup on her pancake, trying to play it off, but I noticed it and I want to see that again and again. As we eat, she sneaks in glances at me before she looks down again, blushing, and that shit is adorable.

"So are you single?" I have to ask, because I need to know what fucker I have to kill for letting her sleep in her vehicle.

She sits back in her seat, smirking at me this time. "Why is my boss asking? I didn't know relationship statuses were needed for the job."

Well, she has fucking got me there.

"This is not your boss talking, darlin'." I wink and she rolls her eyes before laughing slightly. She flips her hair over her shoulder and goes back to her food, letting my question hang in the air, killing me.

She wipes the syrup off her bottom lip with her tongue. "Well, if you must know, I'm single."

Chrystal

The second he hears that I'm single, he smiles widely, showing perfectly straight teeth. He takes our garbage and places it in the trash can. I'm confused. Why did he want to know that, and why isn't he saying a word now? He turns to the door. "Wait. Why do you want to know?" I ask him.

He stops and looks at me over his shoulder. "Because you won't be single long." He walks into the garage, leaving his words hanging in the air, throwing me completely off. I stare at the space where he was just standing, completely floored. Did he just say that? I laugh to myself because I kind of liked his attention and it was sweet that he brought me breakfast.

I go back to work, checking to see who I need to call to pick up their vehicles, but the smile doesn't leave my face.

2

CHRYSTAL

LATER THAT NIGHT

I WAVE to all the guys filing out the door to go home, "See you tomorrow!" Torch calls and waves over his shoulder to me.

Just as I'm about to lock the door, Kyle gets off his bike and walks over to me. "Let's go get dinner." He holds out his hand.

I study him. What does he want with me?

"I won't bite," he teases and wiggles his fingers, giving me the choice whether to take his hand.

I shut the door behind me and lock it, and I take his hand. He walks me over to a truck parked at the side of the building. He opens the door for me and I climb inside.

"Maybe I want you to bite."

His mouth opens, his eyes shining with mirth. "Well, darlin', that's good to know." He shuts the door, and I grin at the sight of him walking around the front of his truck.

One part of me realizes I should be nervous because I just met this man and here I am letting him drive me wherever he wants to take me. But I can't bring myself to be scared. Kyle doesn't seem like the type of man that gets off on beating on defenseless women. He is way too fucking badass for that.

It has not slipped past me that he's huge, scary, and covered head to toe in tattoos, but I have a weakness for bad boys. I just need to learn to decipher which ones are douchebags.

"So where are you from?" he asks.

I push my hair over my shoulder. Should I tell him where exactly? I don't see why not. "Maryland."

His eyebrows rise. "Shit, darlin'. Long-ass drive."

That is an understatement.

I loved Texas the second I crossed the state line, but I kept on driving until I got to this cute little town, and I felt safer here than I'd felt anywhere else. This is where I wanted to have my baby.

I roll down the window and let the evening air move through the cab. I close my eyes and rest my head against the seat, relaxing. I rub my belly and just enjoy the moment of being carefree. I need more moments like this.

I'm not even sure how I have hair at this point; I've been so stressed for the last few years of my life. It's just gotten worse since I've been on my own without one single person on this earth who cares about me or loves me.

Kyle pulls up in front of a diner the Devil Souls own. They own almost the whole town. I open my door, and before I can even get out, he takes my hand so I don't fall. "Thank you."

He winks and puts his hand on the small of my back, holding the door open for me.

We get seated away from everyone else. I sit in front of Kyle, and he's facing the room behind me. He hands me a menu off the table, and I take it from him.

Kyle

The way she looks, the way she smiles—she is so effortlessly beautiful.

Right now she thinks all the guys have left work, but that's not the case at all. Torch and some other members of the club are driving her car to her new apartment, which I spent the fucking day setting up for her. Since this town is small, I converted my basement into an apartment for her. She'll have her privacy and her own keys, but she can come upstairs if she wants to.

She may get pissed at me, but I can't stomach the thought of her sleeping in her vehicle—that I can't handle. She's pregnant, and I know deep down no woman would sleep in her vehicle and drive all the way from fucking Maryland to a middle-of-nowhere town for no reason. She's running from something, and it's not fucking safe for her to live in the garage. A window can easily be broken. Hell, so much can go wrong.

"I think I'm going to get a steak." I put the menu on the table, and she closes hers.

"I think I'm just going to get a kid's meal burger."

The fuck?

Ahhh, she thinks she's paying. "Baby, you're not buying. Get a steak, buy everything on the menu, I don't give a fuck." I push her menu back in front of her.

She rolls her eyes. "Whatever you say," she sasses, and I love that shit. I know that deep down she has a whole bunch of attitude waiting to come out.

I chuckle and sit back, looking at her as she studies the menu once again. I know she can feel me staring at her, because I can see the blush covering her cheekbones.

Chrystal

Our food comes, and it takes everything in me not to shove it in my mouth. I ordered a ribeye, a baked potato, fries, and a milkshake. I haven't eaten like this in a very long time. A hamburger from a fast food place has been my meal of choice for the past couple of months. I'm not sure I'll be able to eat another one.

A woman and her toddler are walking toward the restroom. I smile at the baby, who is grinning and trying to run but his little legs are unsteady. My eyes widen when the baby's legs fold under him and he starts to fall face-first onto the ground. I reach out to catch him, but Kyle beats me to it. He scoops the baby up with one arm and hands him to his mother. She thanks him and walks into the bathroom.

I smile at Kyle. "What?" He doesn't look up from his meal. I don't say a word. I want him to look at me. He puts his fork down, his eyebrows arched, finally looking at me.

"You're a hero."

He laughs and shakes his head at me.

We finish our meal, stealing glances at each other. I'm just trying to figure him out, because I'm kind of confused. Is this a date? Okay, that's stupid. I'm pregnant. What man wants a pregnant woman? No one, that's for sure. Plus I'm hiding a shit-ton of stuff. I come with baggage on top of baggage, and not even the strongest man in the world can handle that.

"Ready to go?" he asks and throws down cash for the food.

"Yeah." I slide to the edge of the booth, and he takes my hand and helps me out of the seat. "Thank you. Has anyone ever told you you're a perfect gentleman, Kyle?"

He gives me a little side grin "Our secret, yeah?" he whispers like it's the biggest secret in the world.

I roll down my window again on the ride back to the garage. Soon I'll be back in the hot hell of my car. Texas heat isn't for the faint of heart, and I would kill for an air conditioner. I would sleep naked if I weren't afraid of someone seeing me.

As the garage comes into view, dread starts to fill me. I sit up in my seat, preparing to get out, but he doesn't pull into the parking lot.

"Uhhh, there was my car," I tell him and laugh slightly, trying to hide my nervousness.

"I didn't see a car."

I eye him like he has a third eye; did he just kidnap me? He just grins like this is the best fucking day of his life.

"Okay, Kyle. Ha ha. Very funny." I laugh and nudge him with my elbow, but he doesn't say shit to me.

I scratch my head, trying to wrap my head around the fact that I have the shittiest luck known to man and I've just been kidnapped, by my boss no less. I mean who else, right? At least I got a steak dinner out of it.

I nod. "Well, what made you wake up today and think to yourself, 'Hey, I'm going to kidnap that pregnant chick that works for me'?" I rub my hands down my legs, trying to hide the fact that I'm nervous. I look over at him. "I mean, I kind of want to know what it is about me that made you think, 'Hey that chick is a good prospect to kidnap.'" He laughs loudly. I mean, a head-thrown-back, hand-resting-on-his-stomach, almost-in-full-convulsions type of laugh.

Well, at least he can laugh, so he can't be too much of a crazy, right? He hits a bump, and the console in front me opens and I see a bottle of lotion.

Oh my god.

"I won't put the lotion on my skin!" I scream and throw the lotion at him. It hits him on the shoulder, bounces off, and hits me on the leg. I grab it and throw it out the window.

"Let me out of this fucking truck or I will give you the biggest titty twister ever!" I scream and shake my fist at him.

I'm pretty sure that Kyle is in tears of laughter at this point. We pull off the main highway. "Oh god, you're going to put me in a hole and make me rub lotion on my skin."

"Chill the fuck out, woman," Kyle manages to get out as he puts the truck in park.

"Look, there's your fucking car." He points to the front of the house, and I see that my car is parked there.

"Well how the fuck did it end up here? Trying to hide the evidence, huh?" I eye him, waiting for him to make his move.

One thing about me is that I've never lost my fire. I may have pretended or played innocent, just because it was easier, but that didn't mean the fire inside me wasn't burning to come out. Oh, I waited, and I can't wait for the fucking day when my husband is at my mercy. I want him to be my bitch. I want him to be helpless to fight back as I kick him while he's down. But I'm also not stupid. I know when to fight and when to run. I had to run.

"Come on, I want to show you something. I promise you I'm not here to hurt you, darlin'. I would never fucking do that, and I sure as fuck wouldn't let anyone else hurt you." He leans over and touches my cheek, and his voice gets deeper, scarier. "I would rip a fucker to pieces if they dared."

I nod and he gets out of the truck, leaving me reeling at his words. I never expected that. He opens the door for me, and I look at my car as I pass. It's the same as it was before. Shitty. We walk to the side of the house, and he unlocks the door. He turns on the light. There are two sets of stairs. One leads upstairs and the other goes to the basement. I step back when he starts in the direction of the basement, and he holds out his hand. "Trust me?" I let out a deep breath as I think it over; then I put my hand in his and decide to throw caution to the wind. I don't miss the satisfied look on his face as I let him lead me down the stairs. He takes out another set of keys and unlocks the door at the bottom of the stairs.

He pushes the door open, and I'm greeted with a cute little apartment. The first thing I see is a leather couch and a flat-screen TV. On one side of the room is a kitchen. It's small but equipped with new appliances. Behind the cozy living room area is a bedroom. It's adorable. I love it. "Is this where you live?" I ask.

He shakes his head and turns my hand over, placing the keys inside it. "This is where you live."

My stomach, my heart, all of it drops to the floor right there.

I laugh nervously. "I swear I just thought I heard you say that I live here."

He leans against the kitchen bar, with two stools under it. "You heard me right. I live upstairs, but you have your keys and you have the only set of keys to get into the basement."

I rub my forehead as I try to process what's happening right now. "Please explain to me."

"Darlin', I can't let you stay in your car another night. This is yours as long as you want it." My stomach twists at his words. He knew I was staying in my car, and I'm embarrassed.

"Is this why you're doing this, you feel sorry for me?" Shame burns deep inside me.

He shakes his head and puts his hand on my face, rubbing his thumb across my cheekbone. "No, darlin', it's not because I feel sorry for you. Get that shit out of your head right now. I will not let a woman of mine sleep inside her car. You may not be ready to hear that, but fuck rules, I will prove that shit to you." I just stare at him; that's all I can do. "I also know shit is going on with your life, and you will share that with me when you're ready. I'll be upstairs if you need me. I'll let you get used to your new home." He leaves just like that, leaving me standing here, mind blown and panties destroyed at his alpha-male words. I look at the stairs he just went up. I am so fucked.

3

CHRYSTAL

I FIND my bags waiting for me on the couch and the kitchen fully stocked with food. I want to cry at the amount of food I have. I know it might seem stupid to some, but if you had barely eaten for a long time, you would understand. And I relish small comforts: being cool when it's hot and warm when it's cold.

I take my bags into my bedroom. Wow. My bedroom. I stare at the white duvet and soft pillows on the bed, and it hits me that he's gone through a lot of trouble to make this place comfortable for me.

I wonder if he has a washing machine I can use? I'll walk up and ask him after I shower.

I spend way too long in the shower, letting the water beat down on my back, loosening the sore muscles I have accumulated from sleeping crouched in the car. I let my hair hang down my back, the ends touching my butt. It's grown so much during my pregnancy.

I need to go to a doctor before I skip town again. I've only gone a couple of times since I got pregnant. I also need to ask Kyle about the rent and utilities since I'll be living here. I gather up the clothes I have to wash and make my way upstairs.

KYLE

I try to calm my nerves as I knock on the door and wait for him to open it. A little bit later he opens the door. "Hi, I just wanted to see if you have a washing machine I can use?" I lift my basket. He waves me inside, and I follow him through the house. It's beautiful and modern, mostly white with some black. It's such a beautiful house for a man, something I never expected. Most men don't even have furniture, let alone home decor. "Your house is beautiful."

He smiles and picks up a photo of an older man and woman. I can see the resemblance between Kyle and the guy in the photo. "My mom decorated it for me."

"That was sweet." I smile at the thought of his mom fretting over him.

He opens a side door. "This is the laundry room. Feel free to use it anytime, but let me know whenever you need to wash clothes. I'll carry up the basket for you. I don't want you to fall." He takes it from me and places it next to the washer; then he reaches above the washer and hands me the laundry detergent and softener. He really is the sweetest and most thoughtful guy. He does things for me that most men would never even think about. He starts to walk out, but I put my hand on his arm. "I want to ask you about the rent. Can you just take it out of my paycheck?"

His eyes soften. "There is no rent. I want you to take care of yourself and the baby, yeah?" He puts his palm on my stomach, which shocks me. I look down. His hand is huge and covers most of my belly.

"Kyle, I can't ask you to do that," I whisper. My insides are shaking from the overwhelming number of things that have been happening. I have a new home and someone basically taking care of me and treating me so nicely. No one has ever treated me like this. I'm sure this is normal for most people, but having someone thinking of my needs is something new. "I don't know what to say," I say softly.

"Don't say anything, sweetheart. If you want to do something for me, you can watch a movie with me?" he suggests.

I smile widely. "I would love that. Let me put my clothes in to wash. Do you have any you want me to throw in with mine?"

"You don't have to do that."

I tilt my head, eyeing him. He laughs and motions to his basket.

"Thank you, Kyle," I call as he walks out of the room.

Kyle

I am a fucking pussy. It thrilled me that she came upstairs to ask me for something. It was my hope that since she would be living downstairs, she would spend the majority of her time upstairs with me.

I just ordered us a pizza and some cheese sticks to be delivered, and I pull up some movies for rent so she can choose. I grab some drinks from the kitchen and place them on the coffee table.

She walks into the living room, and she looks cute in her sweatpants and T-shirt. Her hair is wet and hanging down to her butt. Her hair is a natural, beautiful blonde. "What movie do you want to watch?" I ask her as she sits beside me, curling her legs under her.

"Anything but romantic stuff I'm fine with."

I look at her like she has two heads. "You're the first woman I have ever seen that doesn't love romantic movies."

She laughs and shrugs, turning her attention to the TV, dismissing me. I put in an action movie, make her a plate, and hand it to her. She barely looks at me, deep in her thoughts. I can tell something is bothering her; she has ghosts in her eyes. She's looking at the TV, but I can tell her mind isn't into it. She's being haunted.

Chrystal

Why do I do this to myself? Just a few simple words and I'm depressed. I think back to the bad things that happened.

Romance? I never experienced that. I have never even been properly kissed. I was never raped—I had sex willingly because I thought that was what I had to do as a wife—but I never enjoyed it. And we never really kissed. His lips would brush mine in passing before he would roll off of me and we would go to sleep. That was my life. I lived every single day getting beaten over things that just didn't make sense. How could I do things the way he wanted when he just made things up as he went? It was so hard. Life was just hell. I never slept a full night until I was out on the road by myself and knew that I wouldn't be woken up in the middle of the night to him finding something else wrong.

"Honey?" Kyle touches my shoulder, and I finally snap myself out of my thoughts, before I get buried so deep that it would take me days to get out.

I smile, pushing wet strands of hair behind my ear. "Yeah?" Trying to play it off.

His eyes search my face. "You okay?" he asks, and I nod, putting on a smile because what else can I say? I have not voiced my past to anyone. My own family can't even accept me; how can someone else? I just can't right now. I think I need the chance to accept it myself first before I let anyone else in.

I wave my hand. "I'm fine." I lean over and take a slice of pizza, trying to make it less awkward. He takes a long drink of his beer, and I know it's forgotten when he turns on the movie. I kind of feel bad in a way because he's been so kind to me without asking for anything in return, but how do you start talking about something so painful?

I sit back, pulling my feet up under me, turning my attention to the movie. I just want to enjoy the moment. An hour into the movie, I'm hyperaware of Kyle sitting next to me. We're just an inch apart, and my hand is right next to his on the couch. I feel like I'm in high school and I'm waiting for my crush to hold my hand for the very first time. I feel Kyle laughing beside me. I peek over and he's grinning at the TV like it's the best thing he's ever seen. I'm taken aback at how beautiful his smile is, but I won't be fooled by that. He has this very dangerous edge to him; he's a dangerous man without a doubt. Without thinking, I stick my pinky out, wrapping it around his. I don't look at him. I just pretend that I don't notice it at all. I just want to touch him. I don't care if it's just this. He has been so kind to me today. He pulls his pinky from mine, and I look down just as he intertwines our fingers. I smile happily. This is much better.

The movie ends way too soon. "I guess I'd better get some sleep." He nods and helps me off of the couch. I rub my belly, feeling her or him kick.

"Is it the baby?" He nods toward my stomach.

"You want to feel?" I ask him. He smiles, and I reach forward and take his hand, placing it on my belly where the baby is kicking. His eyes widen in wonder, and looks at my stomach like the baby is going to jump out and snatch him.

"That's amazing."

It is amazing. It's hard to believe that I'm carrying a baby in my body. The miracle of life is so amazing.

"I'll help you down the stairs, don't want you to fall." He takes my hand again, intertwining our fingers, and walks me down the stairs. I feel special. I know it's stupid and he's just being nice. That's all this can be. I'm pregnant, very pregnant. Me being attractive flew out the window a few months ago. I push open my door and step inside, looking back at Kyle.

"Goodnight," I say softly, smiling.

"Goodnight darlin'."

I pull the door shut, my eyes closed. I let out a deep breath and walk to my bedroom, ready to sleep for days.

4

CHRYSTAL

ONE WEEK LATER

"Darlin', your appointment is at four, right?" Kyle asks, sticking his head in the door.

"Yes, it's right around the corner."

This past week has been heaven on earth compared to living in the backseat of my car. I'm now getting adjusted to staying with Kyle, and we have become best friends, honestly. Ones that flirt relentlessly with each other. He winks and leaves me alone once again, and my stomach twists. God, why does he have to be so attractive?

I go back to my work, ordering parts for the guys. Today is the first appointment I could get to see the doctor. I'm excited to find out if I'm having a girl or a boy, but I feel kind of bad that I haven't seen a doctor in such a long time. That's kind of hard to do when you don't have insurance.

Kyle has decided he must drive me everywhere, which I don't mind at all because I'm so sick and tired of my car.

The back door bursts open and I spin around, confused, because no one ever uses this door. Some man I've never seen before steps inside the office, clawing his skin until it bleeds.

"Are you okay, sir?" I ask. His eyes snap to mine. His eyes are blood red, and I know instantly that he's on something. I also know that I'm in danger because he doesn't look like he's in his right mind.

I clear my throat and try to make myself as friendly as possible. I'm beating myself up because I should have locked the door. I'm not even sure how he got past the guys in the first place. I push myself away from my desk so I can run if I need to. "Why don't you sit down there, sir, and I'll help you in a second." I motion to the seat beside me. He just continues to stare at me.

I reach under the desk and hit the alert button the guys installed a few days ago in case of an emergency. He doesn't move, he doesn't even blink, and saliva is dripping from the side of his mouth. One second he is stoical, the next he's running straight for me. I scream and push my chair at him as hard as I can, throwing him off balance. I run out the door into the main garage with him close behind me. Fear is lodged deep in my throat, not allowing me to scream.

I look around for someone to help me, and Kyle runs into the building. His eyes narrow, and I turn around just as the crazy guy reaches for my hair. Kyle is there in a second, and his hand closes around my assailant's hand. Kyle all but picks me up to put me behind him, and I stare in shock as I see Kyle in a whole different light. He picks up the guy and slams him face-down onto the concrete floor. I wince at the crunching sound the second his face connects.

"What the fuck do you think you're doing?" Kyle growls, pushing his face harder against the floor. Blood pools around the guy's face. Torch comes in and pulls me farther away from the scene playing out just a few feet in front of me.

"I need it!" the crazy guy screams from the ground, trying to push Kyle off of him. My eyes widen at the sight of him screaming, kicking, and clawing the ground.

Kyle closes his eyes, shaking his head. "I can't fucking help you, Phillip. We have told you one hundred times we don't sell that shit here! Now you've fucked up. You've decided to come after a woman. A woman in this club, as a matter of fact."

Phillip stops moving and his eyes connect with mine. I can see the deep-rooted fear in them. Kyle looks over at two guys wearing cuts in the corner of the room. The patches on their cuts say "Prospect." They reach down and carry Philip out of the room kicking and screaming. Kyle walks over to me. "Are you okay, darlin'?" His face is full of concern, and he touches my face tenderly.

I smile. I can't help it; he's being so sweet right now. "I'm fine, he just startled me is all."

Kyle drags his hands from my face, down my arms, to my hands. "Good, that just saved his fucking life." His face is tight with anger at the thought of Phillip hurting me. Wait, what?

Kyle walks me back into my office, helps me sit down, and locks the back door. "I am going to get a fucking better alarm system installed. This shit won't ever happen again," he spits out, glaring at the door like it's the cause of all of his problems. He takes out his phone. "You know what to do. I'll be there in five minutes." He puts his phone in his pocket and turns to me. "Are you sure you're okay?"

I laugh. "Yes, honey, I'm fine. He's just a sick man. He needs his ass beat and then rehab."

His face lightens, grinning. "I plan on doing one of those. I'll be back to take you to your appointment. Techy, get your ass in here and watch over Chrystal!" Kyle yells, and one of the prospects walks back into the room and sits down in the chair across from me. I stare at Kyle's back, watching him leave, then I look at Techy, who is busy typing away on his phone. I guess that's where he got his name from.

Kyle

I walk into the clubhouse, where they have Phillip sitting in a chair waiting for the ass beating he's going to get from me.

Usually I would let that shit go, but he was planning on hurting Chrystal, and that is fucking unacceptable. I saw red seeing her run from her office with that fucker on her tail, trying to grab her.

I can taste the rage, every single cell in my body screaming at me to fucking tear him to bits. My urge to protect her is in every single part of my being.

Phillip starts screaming when he sees me walking toward him. "I'm sorry, she looked like she had money, I needed it," he begs, like that is going to help his case.

I shake my head at his stupidity. He's not worth a single ounce of my breath. He closes his eyes just as my fist plows into his nose. How I fucking love the feel of a nose breaking underneath my fist.

I'm not going to kill him. I'm just going to make him wish that I had. Everyone needs to fucking know, no one messes with the Devil Souls MC and our women.

Chrystal

I'M NERVOUS WAITING FOR THE DOCTOR TO SHOW UP. I KIND OF expected Kyle to sit in the waiting room, but he's still next to me, holding my hand. I'm a selfish woman. I want to pretend we're married and having a baby together. That would be perfect. I can dream.

There's a knock at the door before the doctor steps into the room. "It's nice to meet you, Chrystal. I'm Shelia." I shake her hand, smiling back at her. She seems sweet. "You ready for your ultrasound?" she asks, pulling my shirt up off my belly and

KYLE

tucking it under my bra. "Do you want to find out what you're having today?" She sits down in her chair, placing the doppler against my stomach. My eyes are glued to the screen, waiting impatiently to see my baby.

"I would love that." A *whoosh-whoosh* fills the room, and it's the most beautiful sound. The sound of my baby's heartbeat. The doctor studies the screen for a few minutes. I can't make out much of the image. She grins before pointing to something on the screen. "Looks like you're having a girl." My heart swells at the thought of having a precious little angel. My eyes don't leave the screen, eating up every second I have to see her.

"She's going to beautiful like her momma," Kyle tells me and I look over at him. That was so incredibly sweet. Sheila prints off some pictures for me to keep, and I hand them to Kyle as I wipe off my belly and fix my clothes.

"I'll have someone call you with your next appointment," Sheila says. "Have a nice evening!"

I slide off the bed with Kyle's help. "Thank you for being here with me. You didn't have to be." I take hold of his forearm.

He rolls his eyes. "I know I didn't have to be. I want to be here." He holds the door open for me, and I can't help but smile. His hand goes to the small of my back. He is majorly protective. I've noticed that a lot since I moved in with him. While we were in the waiting room, a man sat down next to me, and Kyle picked me up and moved me closer to him. I won't lie and say I didn't enjoy that. It makes me feel safe. I haven't experienced that much in my life, so I'm basking in it.

"Want to go to the baby store?" Kyle asks once we're in the truck.

"Yes!"

He laughs and drives me across town to the baby store. Now that I have a place to stay and money in my pocket, I can buy the things I need. I'm coming to the decision that I need to tell Kyle the truth. I want to tell him what caused me to run, because he deserves that after all he has done for me, plus I'm growing to trust him. Before I know it, we're parked, and Kyle comes around the front of the truck to help me out. He pulls open my door, and as he drags his hands down my body, to my waist, my breath stills at his touches. As he lifts me down, my hands go to his shoulders, and I don't let go, even when my feet are planted on the ground.

"Chrystal," Kyle says just before both of his hands go to my cheeks, before his mouth connects with mine. I groan as he doesn't just kiss me, he takes my mouth. My heart is beating so hard I'm sure he can feel it. I shiver and bring my hands from his shoulders to the back of his head, brushing my fingers in his hair.

He finally breaks the kiss, resting his forehead against mine as we both try to catch our breath. That's the kind of kiss every woman wants and the one that changes her life forever. "Wow," I whisper.

He laughs silently, kissing me once more on the lips sweetly. "Come on, let's go shop for our angel." I let him lead me into the store, still in a daze. I guess I was wrong. Maybe he is attracted to me.

Chrystal

OUR SHOPPING TRIP WENT VERY WELL, AND I THINK KYLE WAS just as excited as I was. He bought her a tiny pair of a biker boots and a Harley shirt that he just had to have. We bought a ton of things, but I still have a lot more to get: a crib, a bassinet, and other furniture.

Now I'm downstairs in my apartment, trying to talk myself out of telling Kyle about my past. I'm married, and that is a hard pill to swallow. I'm scared to see his reaction when he learns that fact, along with the other things that went on. I shake my hands, trying to stop them from trembling, close my eyes, and say a little prayer before I swing the door open and make my way up the stairs to his part of the house.

I knock on the door gently, one part of me hoping that he doesn't hear me. Maybe I can get by for one more night.

The door swings open, and Kyle is standing in front of me wearing a pair of gray sweats and a white T-shirt that does amazing things for him. "Come on in, you don't even have to knock, Chrystal." He gives me a look telling me not to argue with him.

I laugh, holding up my hands. "Fine." I'm not going to argue with that. My smile drops the second I think about why I'm up here in the first place.

Kyle notices and studies me. "What the fuck is the matter?"

I let out a deep breath, gathering every single bit of courage I have. "I need to tell you the reason why I was sleeping in my car."

His eyes widen in realization, and he takes my hand and walks with me to the living room. I sit on the couch and grab the blanket off the back like it's going to protect me somehow, keep me grounded. I've only told one person about him, about how he treated me—she threw me out on my ass.

Kyle sits in front of me, fully facing me.

"I was married when I was eighteen years old," I start off, and Kyle's eyes jump. "When I was sixteen years old, my mother introduced me to the man; his name was Joshua Campbell. I was to marry when I graduated from high school. He was twenty-eight when I met him, and he was thirty when I married him." Kyle's face darkens, jaw tight. "I didn't want to marry him, but in exchange for me, my mother would be living a life of luxury." I feel bitter at the thought of my mother doing this to me and the fact that I was stupid enough to follow through with it, but I was so young. "The marriage wasn't bad at first, then the real side of him slipped out when I accidentally spilled his plate of food. That was the first time he hit me." I whisper the last part, ashamed. "I went to my mother, hoping she would take me in, but she threw me out because she didn't want to lose her lifestyle. My father is so brainwashed by my mother, he doesn't know the sky from the ground." I pull the blanket farther up my arms, chilled to the bone. "So I picked myself up and went back to him, promising myself I would save money so I could run."

I don't look at Kyle because I can't handle that right now, and I need to finish this. "It got worse. He would find things that didn't make any sense, and I would get beaten. He broke my toes because I left my shoes out and he tripped over them." The memories of all of this are overwhelming. I never got to deal with everything.

I finally look at Kyle. "I found out I was pregnant, so I had to get out. I bought a broken-down car with cash, I got in, and I never looked back. Here I am. Roseville, Maryland is a place I never want to see again," I whisper.

Kyle reaches out to touch my face but stops himself. "I will not touch you when I have such fucking anger inside me. He is going to pay. He is never going to hurt you ever again."

But that doesn't mean I can't touch him. I crawl over to him, lifting my leg over his and hugging him tightly. He hesitates to hold me for a second before he gives in, burying his face deep in my shoulder. I close my eyes and just bask in the feeling of being safe. "Chrystal," Kyle says, and when I lift my head to look at him, he puts his hand on my neck. "If you had one fucking wish when it comes to that bastard, what would it be?"

I think on it, but there is one thing I wished over and over as he beat me down and hurt me. "I want him to die. When he was hurting me, belittling me, I wished him dead so many times," I admit, not even caring if it makes me a bad person. Kyle smiles. He smiles in a way that sends shivers down my spine. He doesn't say a word; he just holds me. I fall asleep in his arms, the best sleep I've had in years.

Kyle

I wait until she falls asleep, and I carry her upstairs to my bed. I don't want to be apart from her right now. I just want to fucking look at her and make sure she's okay. The pain I saw on her face as she relived in her mind the horrors that fucker inflicted upon her, that shit will haunt me. How a fucking man can lay hands on a woman, I will never fucking fathom, but I have one thing in store for him. I pick up my phone and call Torch. "Call and charter the jet. We're going to Maryland."

5

KYLE

I LEFT Texas at five o'clock in the morning. Techy is staying with Chrystal while I'm gone.

I woke her up and told her I was leaving for a day or two on a business trip. She nodded and smiled her beautiful smile. It killed me to leave her in my bed, but I need to take care of this so she can live her life without the fear of him finding her.

When I pull through the gate at the airport, Torch, Ryan, Jack, and Butcher are already waiting to board the plane. These men are my brothers. They don't even know why we're going to Maryland, but they're fucking here and ready.

They follow me onto the plane, we get seated, and they stare at me, waiting for me to reveal the purpose of our trip. "Chrystal told me why she was running and sleeping in her car. She's on the run from a man she was forced to marry when she turned eighteen years old. He fucking beat her every day, so I'm going to take care of this shit." I grit out the last part through my teeth. The thought of someone touching her that way fucking kills me. All of the guys' faces show shock and resignation because it just became everyone's mission.

We all sit in silence, deep in our thoughts. I take out my phone and text Chrystal; she should be getting up any minute.

"Good morning, darlin'."

"Good morning, handsome." I don't even bother trying to stop the smile she brings.

"Brother has it bad," Torch teases me, and I laugh along with the rest of them, because I don't care. I look Torch straight in the eye. "Wait until the day she comes crashing into your life, everything will change."

He nods, settling back in his seat.

All my brothers are at a point in their lives where they want to settle down. We have built this fucking empire just for us and our future generations. We wanted something to pass down to our kids and their kids. This is why we busted our asses for so many years.

We arrive in Maryland. Techy texted me the addresses for Mr. Fucking Joshua and Chrystal's mother—I plan to pay her father a visit too. You're supposed to protect your daughter, and he did none of that.

We have an SUV waiting for us at the airport. First we check into our hotel and grab a late lunch. A couple of hours later, we pull up in front of Joshua's place. Techy has hacked into the cameras inside his house, and Joshua is there right now, talking to a private investigator about how to find Chrystal.

We wait until he gets off the phone before we get out of the SUV. Ryan goes to the back of the house to make sure Joshua doesn't try to run out the back before we get inside. Butcher, Torch and I take the front of the house. We walk up and ring the doorbell, my fingers itching to wrap around his neck. We're going to be the last people he's ever going to fucking see. He's going to die knowing that I'm going to take care of his baby and marry his wife. I will do it fucking smiling.

He opens the door, and he takes a step back when he sees the three of us, so I give him the thing he wants most of all. "I know the location of your wife."

His eyes widen before he grins. I can see why he has everyone fooled. He is put together. His pearly white grin must make everyone think he's a fucking good ole boy.

He takes a step back, naïvely allowing us inside his house. Butcher shuts the door behind him, standing in front of it.

"Come on, boys, tell me how you know my wife." He leads us into the living room.

I see a camera in the corner of the room, and I smile into it, knowing Techy is watching. I make up a bullshit story. "Your private investigator got a hold of some people we know. She works for us and we connected the dots." His face darkens as he looks at all of us. We aren't wearing our cuts because this isn't our state.

"Works for you how?" he asks slowly, cracking the side of his neck, as his face reddens more and more.

I lift my arms, smirking. "For the club."

He jumps to his feet. "She's a stripper?" he screams, pacing in front of me without looking at us. "That stupid bitch. Apparently the lessons I taught her didn't fucking stick!"

I laugh, because he is utterly fucking pathetic. The brothers join in with me. He doesn't know us, and we come here telling him we know his wife? How gullible is he?

He glares at all of us. "I don't get what's so funny."

I look him dead in the eye. "You are."

His eyes narrow on me, his face turning even redder, as he points to himself. "Me?" he yells.

I nod. "Yeah, you motherfucker. You're the one who's pathetic." I sit farther back on his couch, getting comfortable. "We tell you we know your wife, and *bam*, here we are in your house."

He takes a step back, looking at all of us as it starts to sink in. Surprise, fucker, we aren't your saving grace.

"Why are you here then?" he asks, his voice calmer.

I grin. "Did I mention your wife is living with me?" His eyes widen. "Last night she told me some things about you, how you liked to beat her over everything and made her suffer every day."

His lips start to shake as he takes another step back, running straight into Butcher, who grunts, kicking him right behind the knee. The fucker falls to the ground.

I grip his face. "Ding, ding, ding, you're connecting the dots. I'm not here to give her to you. I'm here to kill you." I laugh, watching him shake. "You're going to die knowing your wife is going to be mine, your daughter in her belly is going to be mine." I grin, watching the tears fill his eyes.

I squeeze his face tighter. "Your tears mean shit to me. How many times did she cry and ask you not to hurt her?" He looks at the ground, and I shake his face. "Tell me," I demand.

"Almost every day," he whispers. Then he raises his head. "She deserved it."

I point my finger in his face. "Ah, ah, ah, no matter what she did. You're a grown-ass man, what could she have done to deserve to be hurt? Absolutely nothing." I can't stand a woman beater, but one thing is weighing on my mind.

"Did you rape her?" I don't want to fucking know, but I need to know.

His eyes widen. "No, I never raped her. She never fucking enjoyed it if that's what you're asking. She's defective or something, wasn't a good lay." He gloats at the last part.

I let go of his face, giving him a push. He makes me sick. The fucking sight of him disgusts me to the point I want to vomit.

I look at Butcher, who hands me a gun with a silencer. Joshua starts to scream and I roll my eyes. "Shut up, screaming does nothing but make you look even more pathetic, if that's even possible."

He shuts up and I laugh. "Any last words before I go home?" I smirk, seeing the anger in his eyes. He's trying to play innocent so I won't kill him.

Nothing can stop me from ending his life. Picturing her being hurt replays over and over in my head. "Did you know what her wish was? She wants you dead. Her wish is coming true."

I can see the disbelief written on his face. He tried to break her because his ego needed her to be broken so he could be full of himself. He's nothing but a waste of space. I press the gun to his face and, without blinking, flinching, or a second of guilt, I pull the trigger, ending his life, ending Chrystal's torment. His body hits the floor with a thump.

We'll just leave his body here, because he isn't even worth the trouble of burying him. I hand Butcher back the gun, and we walk out of the house. One major perk is it's in the middle of nowhere, which makes it easier to cover our tracks or just sneak in and out without anyone noticing.

We pull up in front of a trailer park, and I take great pleasure in knowing that when Chrystal left, Joshua didn't give her parents money anymore. It fucking floors me that they gave their daughter away to someone who was a monster so they could live a better life. I'd rather starve to fucking death than allow any of mine to go without or suffer an ounce of pain.

The moment everyone in the trailer park spots our SUV, they take off running and disappear inside their homes. Ryan goes to the back of the trailer while three of us knock on the door, exactly how we approached Josh. A woman opens the door. She looks exactly like Chrystal, which hits me right in the gut, but I notice the difference right off the bat. Her eyes are dead; she has no life inside her.

"Can I help you?" she snaps, eyeing me like I'm the cause of all of her problems. I push the door open, making my way inside her trailer, and step past her. I make sure not to touch her. I don't want her fucking evil filth on me.

I look around and notice how filthy the place is; trash is piled all around the room. Chrystal's father is sitting on the couch, not even bothering to look at us.

"Richard!" Chrystal's mother yells and walks over to him.

Then he glares at her. "What do you want, Casey?" I can see the hate written all over his face. Then he looks over and sees all of us.

"These men just busted in the house!" she screeches, like she isn't standing right in front of him.

He stands up and faces us. "What do you want?"

"Your daughter—" I start, but he holds his hand up.

"I am not telling you shit. I didn't even know my daughter was being forced to marry that stupid motherfucker until my wife told me we had to leave our apartment. Nor did I know he fucking beat her until I saw a doctor's report sitting on his desk." He takes a step toward me, his eyes bloodshot. "Please kill me. I don't deserve to live, not after I let shit happen, right under my nose, to my baby girl. For years I allowed myself to be used and abused by this bitch standing behind me."

I was not expecting that. I assumed he and his wife were equally responsible for what happened to Chrystal. I had no idea he was an abused man who has been stuck in hell for a very long time. That doesn't discount the fact that he let this stuff happen. But I think he's suffering enough as it fucking is. I can see the pain written all over him.

"Now I can't find her. I want to find her so I can apologize to her for failing her as a father." I can see tears in his eyes.

I look at Torch and he shrugs. "Watch them," I tell the guys, and I step out onto the porch to call Chrystal.

"Hello?"

"Hey baby." I instantly feel better just hearing her voice.

"How's the trip? Where are you, by the way?" she asks.

One part of me doesn't want to tell her, but I need to see if she's strong enough to be a part of the MC. She can be a part of the MC and be blind to it or she can stand by my side because that's what I want from her. "Maryland."

She gasps and a door slams shut. My guess is that she's shutting her office door so nobody can eavesdrop. It's silent for a few beats before she finally speaks. "Did you?" she whispers.

I stare out across the park and let out a deep breath. "Kill him? Yeah I did, angel." I lay it all out for her.

My phone starts vibrating. I look at the screen and see it's a FaceTime call from Chrystal. I answer it and sit on the edge of the porch so I can talk to her. She has tears in her eyes and is holding her stomach.

"Are you okay?" I ask. I don't want to lose her before I even have her.

It may be stupid, it may make me a pussy, but this girl could own all of me, and I knew it the second I saw her sitting at her desk in my garage.

She laughs, wiping her tears. "Am I okay? I'm amazing right now. Do you know how it feels to be able to breathe and not be scared, Kyle? My baby will be safe." Her voice softens at the last part.

Fuck me, I just can't… Seeing those tears in her eyes. "Don't cry, baby." I want to reach through the screen and wipe away her tears.

"I may be crazy to be so relieved, but I really am, Kyle. I never thought for a second you would hop on a plane to Maryland the very next morning." She laughs and holds her stomach, her smile doing shit to my heart.

"I have one more question, baby. Your dad? How did you feel about him?" His words don't mean shit to me until she gives me the go-ahead.

She settles back in her seat. "My dad is fucked up because my mother did that to him. He used to be a really great dad back in the day, but he stayed away from home more and more because she is just awful. I'm not mad at him. I don't blame him. He could have done better, but he's the only parent I ever had. He took care of me when I was little, my mother did nothing. He didn't know she was forcing me to marry him. She kind of used my dad as an excuse, because he worked so hard." She looks behind me. "Wait, you're at our old house."

I nod. "I was coming here to beat the shit out of your dad, but then I noticed that he wasn't the real devil…it was your mother."

"My mother is pure evil, she doesn't have one ounce of goodness in her heart. I wish my father were away from her so he could manage to start over and maybe be happy, maybe even be in the baby's life. Maybe I can build some type of relationship with him."

I smile because I can make that happen. "You got it, babe. You want to talk to him?"

She smiles widely. "Yes, please."

I take the phone inside the house with me. Richard is still standing next to the guys. Casey is hovering in the back of the living room, pretending to be scared, but I don't think she can summon up that emotion.

"Daddy?" Chrystal says, and Richard's head snaps to my phone. Casey gasps and takes out her phone, probably to call Joshua. I smirk at that.

"Baby girl?" Richard takes the phone from me, and I watch it all play out. "You okay, honey? Do you need anything?" he asks.

"I'm fine, Dad. I'm living with Kyle. He's taking really good care of me. The best." Well shit if it didn't make me feel a hundred feet tall when she said that. Richard looks at me and smiles. I want to rip the phone out of his hand so I can talk to her again.

"Let me have it," I ask, almost nicely. He hands me the phone.

"Angel, I'll call you later. I got shit to settle." She smiles and hangs up. I slip my phone in my pocket and look at her father—then her mother, which makes me want to puke.

37

"Richard, it seems to me that it's your lucky day. Chrystal said she wished she could have her dad in her life, in our baby's life, in hopes of rebuilding your relationship. I'm offering you a choice to stay with us at the hotel and get on the jet with us tomorrow. I will help you find a place and a job and get your life in order."

I step closer to him, getting in his face. "If you take the offer, you will crawl on your hands and fucking knees and bend over backwards to be there for her and be what she wants." I smile, loving seeing the fear in his face. "If you don't, I will end you. You will be right back here with that fucking witch, which I'm sure would be worse than death."

"Richard, please don't do this to me." The witch slithers her way up to Richard and wraps her arm around his back. "Why don't you take me with you, and I can be a good mother."

I laugh, because that is the dumbest thing I have heard in my life. I arch an eyebrow at Richard.

"I take the offer."

I smile and then I look at her. "You don't ask shit of me. I don't even want to look at you, and you better be fucking glad you're a woman because, luckily for you, I don't hurt women. Gather your shit, Richard." He walks to the back of the house, and I go outside with a mission in mind.

I spot a woman with a permanent scowl on her face, who looks like she could even beat me up. "Come here," I tell her and she makes her way over. "How much would it take for you to beat up the bitch in that trailer after we leave?"

Her eyes widen before she grins. "Shit, I hate that bitch. I'll take five hundred because I have kids to feed."

I take out my wallet and hand her five hundred along with a cell phone. "If you send me pictures, I'll give you a hundred more. If you torment her a little every week or so, and provide proof, I'll send you more."

"Fuck yeah, you got it!" She takes the money.

"Make sure you don't kill her though," I call out, and she waves her hand over her shoulder. Well, I tried.

Thirty minutes later Richard returns from the back of the house. Casey is still sitting on the couch staring at the wall. I guess she's finally realizing she's going to have to take care of herself for the first time in her life.

"Ready?" I ask Richard.

He nods and walks to the door without even looking in Casey's direction.

"Please don't leave me, Richard. I am your family," she yells, finally getting up and walking toward him.

He shakes his head. "You're not my family, Chrystal is." At that he steps out onto the porch.

"Have fun, bitch." I smirk at her, leaving her standing alone, and the guys follow me out to the SUV, where Richard is already waiting for us.

She watches us leave, and I take sick satisfaction in the fact that she's going to suffer. She has lost everything and is going to be alone. The way she failed Chrystal, she deserves it.

I unlock the SUV. My skin is crawling from being in that fucking pigsty but, most of all, I am more than ready to be home with Chrystal. Just as I'm pulling out of the driveway, in the mirror, I see the woman I paid stepping inside the trailer. The day is just getting fucking better.

6

CHRYSTAL

I'm finally home after another day at work. I'm staying upstairs now. I've slept in Kyle's bed every night since he left.

Kyle is coming home from Maryland today with my father. I never expected him to leave my mother. I guess my leaving opened his eyes. My stomach is in knots waiting for Kyle to walk through those doors. I'm more than ready to touch him and breathe in his scent. I never feel more safe than when he is here.

I hear a vehicle outside, and I can't stop the grin that spreads across my face.

The door is unlocked, and when Kyle steps inside the house, it's like I can breathe for the first time since he left. He smiles when he sees me, and it lights up his whole face, showing the softer side of him.

When he said he was leaving on a trip, I never once expected that he was going to Maryland, that he was making my wish come true. That's when I realized how Kyle felt about me. If you don't deeply care for someone, you don't take such extreme measures to protect them. On top of all that, he brought my dad home to me.

He took me in when I was homeless, gave me a job, and has made me so happy. He has made me feel safe, and he has made me start to fall in love for the first time in my life. He has wiped away my tears and seen the absolute worst of me. But he walks into the house with a smile on his face, excited to see me, and my heart is so full that it feels like it's going to burst. Kyle has completely changed my life.

When he walks over to me, I stand up and wrap my arms around him, the smell of him covering me from head to toe, wrapping me in a blanket that feels so safe. Kyle is home. It's not the things he's done for me; it's who he is that makes me feel this way. His arms are wrapped around me tightly, and I'm shaking. He loosens his arms around me, his hand coming around to cup my face. "Why are you shaking? Are you cold?" He rubs my arms.

I smile, shaking my head. "I just missed you," I admit to him. I'm not going to hide myself anymore. All of that went out the window when he took the thing I feared most and ended it.

His face softens, and he closes his eyes and rests his forehead against mine. "I missed you too, sweet girl." His voice is soft. I stand up on the tips of my toes, kissing him while wrapping my arms around his neck. His hands cup my ass, lifting me off the floor and carrying me up the stairs as I kiss him. I love that he is so strong that he can carry me like I weigh nothing.

A minute later, I feel the soft bed at my back as he lays me down gently and stops kissing me. His eyes are filled with need as he looks down at me. "Are you sure?" he asks before even touching me.

I nod, reaching out and intertwining our fingers. "I want you, Kyle." He pulls his shirt over his head, and my eyes feast on his abs.

My god. His body is utter perfection, his skin tan without a blemish. I lean forward, running my hands down his chest to his stomach, stopping right at the top of his belt.

"Raise your arms."

I do as he asks, watching him watch me as he pulls the shirt over my head. He takes me in, he licks his lips, and I shiver at the pure need on his face. I should feel self-conscious right now, I am pregnant, but the way he's looking at me makes me feel like I'm beautiful. He smiles, making his face softer. His fingers push my hair over my shoulders, and he drags them gently down my back and unsnaps my bra. He slides the straps down my arms, freeing me completely. "Perfection," he whispers, dragging his hands down my sides, oh so gently, like he's afraid to touch me.

I am at his mercy. I am surrendering all of myself to him. I am ready. He pulls my shorts down, bringing my panties with them, and he throws them to the floor. "Fuck."

That simple word is my undoing. I smile widely and grab his hands, pulling him to me, kissing him, needing him. He laughs and grips my jaw, kissing me fully, making my toes curl. I run my fingers down his back, loving the feel of his muscles. His mouth drifts down to my neck, and my head tilts instinctually as his lips kiss, lick, and suck tenderly.

This is all new for me. Someone just loving me is something I've never experienced. I bury my hands in his hair, enjoying every single second of this.

He looks up at me, right before his lips wrap around one of my very sensitive nipples. I hiss and arch my back into him, pleasure shooting straight down to my pussy. He lets me go with a pop, swirling his tongue around the tip. I shiver and lift my legs so they're resting on either side of his hips. He grinds himself against me, and I jolt at the sudden pleasure.

Kyle slides off of me and moves toward the end of the bed. He strips himself out of the rest of his clothes. His hands wrap around my thighs, spreading my legs fully, and he's looking at me. I blush deeply, because I have never been this exposed before. I cover my face instinctively.

"Don't hide yourself from me, sweetheart. There has never

been anything more beautiful than you." I can't even stop the tears that fill my eyes at his unbelievably sweet words. I nod, because if I speak I may just cry.

He leans down and kisses my stomach, before he puts his face right above my pussy. I widen my eyes. Is he really going to do what I think he is? At the first lick across my clit, my eyes close because it's something completely new to me. Women have talked about the pleasure you can get from a man, but I never experienced it firsthand.

"Mmm." He moans, opens my lips, and sucks my clit deep into his mouth. My legs shake, and I lift them higher and drape them over his shoulders. He shakes his head, licking all around my clit. I feel him shift and he slips two fingers inside me.

"Oh shit," I hiss as he licks, sucks, and moves his finger in sync, curling. "Oh god, Kyle." I bury my fingers into his hair, loving feeling the movement of his head as he pleasures me. His hands sneak under my ass, lifting me so he can reach me better. My legs are shaking, my whole body tightening, fighting to have my first orgasm. I press my hands against the headboard, bracing myself. "Kyle," I whimper, freezing as my orgasm hits me hard.

"That's right, baby, come for me," he growls, kissing either side of my thighs. I shiver, goosebumps wrecking my whole body. Kyle lowers my legs to the bed, running his hands from the tops of my thighs down to my feet. He crawls up my body, rests his elbows on either side of my face, and kisses me sweetly.

"Ready, angel?" he asks when he pulls back. I nod and spread my legs further for him to fit better between them. I brace myself for the pain, because that always comes. I rest my shaking hands on his shoulders, as the nerves are ready to set in. He studies me, his eyes searching from my face to my hands.

"Why are you shaking?" he asks, resting his forehead against mine. He sneaks an arm between our bodies, his thumb rubbing my clit. My body relaxes instantly.

"Just nervous," I tell him softly, trying not to moan.

"Why are you nervous?" he asks, while continuously working my body, driving me wild.

"It's nothing." I don't want to talk about it, because it could stop him altogether. I pull him down to kiss me, and I feel him pressing against my entrance. He looks into my eye as he slowly, gently sinks inside me. My eyes roll back in my head because the pleasure is not what I'd ever expected. I tilt my hips up so he can go deeper. He is so thick. He drags his tongue up my neck.

"You can move," I whisper.

He scoots his body up, his hands sliding under my butt and thighs, and that's when he first slams inside me.

Oh shit. I open my eyes and he is watching me, his face full of emotion. His hands intertwine with mine, lifting them above my head. With every second, every breath, we are connected on a soul level. My heart fills.

"You are mine, Chrystal. Fully, completely. Every single part of you belongs to me, and the baby inside you will be my daughter."

His eyes convey that he means it, and my lip quivers. "Kyle." I shake my head, overwhelmed with tears, and I slip my hands from his to touch his face. I lean forward, kissing him, my whole body shaking from pleasure and intense emotions. I need to tell him how I feel. I pull back and rub his cheekbones. "I love you, Kyle. I think I've loved you from the second you practically kidnapped me."

He laughs, but I can tell that my words mean a lot to him. He takes my hand in his, resting it against his chest right above his heart. "This is yours, angel. You own all of me."

No more words are spoken, just feelings. Actions speak louder than words, and he loves me in a way that is going to stick with me forever. He may not have been my first, but he is my first lover in all the ways that count. Our eyes never leave each other's as he moves inside me.

He reaches between our bodies, rubbing my clit and moving faster, harder. "Come, angel." He pinches my clit, and I clench down on him hard. I drag my hands down his back to his ass, pulling him as deep inside me as he can go as he comes.

"Fuck," he groans, his face buried in my neck, and he is mindful of my belly. He slowly slides out of me and pulls me into his side, wrapping his arm around me, his hand resting protectively on my belly. Baby girl kicks and bumps Kyle's hands. "Did she just kick me?" he asks in wonder. He sits up, resting his head against my belly. "Kick for me, angel," he whispers to her, rubbing my belly.

I smile watching him, my heart swelling when she kicks again and he smiles so beautifully. "Wow." He kisses the spot where she kicked and closes his eyes. This is absolute heaven. This is everything that I dreamed of, but more than I could have ever imagined.

"What are you thinking of naming her?" he asks, still lying on my belly.

"Cassandra."

He thinks for a moment. "Cassandra, I like it." He smiles and I return it.

Nothing could get better than this.

7

CHRYSTAL

ONE MONTH LATER

Today I am going to see my dad. It's been a long time since I've seen him and I'm nervous.

I'm almost nine months pregnant. I have two weeks to go before my due date, and Kyle has made it his mission to not allow me to lift a finger.

The last month has been all about me and Kyle adjusting to our life together. I haven't stayed in my apartment downstairs since before he left to kill my husband. I am now a widow. They found Joshua's body and someone called to sadly inform me of my husband's death. There are no leads as to what actually killed him. I played the grieving wife, and now I am a very rich woman. I know exactly what I want to do with the money.

I want to open a center for women and men who are in violent relationships. I want to give them a safe haven so they can escape from that horrible situation and get their lives started. I will need houses for them, but I can't do it alone and I think I want the MC to be involved because they protected me. They can help keep the center safe.

But right now I am going to concentrate on seeing my

father. Kyle is driving me to his house. My father already has a place to live, which I'm sure Kyle had a huge play in. He is a fucking badass. I witnessed it firsthand when I accidentally walked in on him getting some information from someone who was trying to sell drugs in town. Not that I ever doubted it. He killed my ex-husband. But seeing it firsthand, and seeing his face, made it real.

He is the president of an MC, but I am not scared of him. He handles me with such tenderness. I am in awe of how he is with me compared to his behavior around others.

We pull up outside a cute white house. A truck is parked outside, and my dad is sitting on the front porch in a rocking chair.

Kyle gets out of the truck and practically lifts me out, because it's hard for me to get out. My dad moves to the edge of the small porch, watching us, and my nose burns with unshed tears because he looks so good. He looks healthy. He looks like the dad I knew when I was little. I walk straight up to him and hug him. He smells the same, but he looks so much better.

"Dad, I missed you," I whisper, and I close my eyes and enjoy the moment. I am so happy that Kyle brought him home, even though I don't have a relationship with him, and it makes me feel better that he has a chance now.

"I missed you too, baby girl." He kisses the top of my head, and we stand in silence together, just taking in the moment. Kyle is right behind me, his hand on the small of my back. He is always ready to protect me, ready to jump at my every need.

"Come on in, I have some dinner ready." He lets me go, smoothing my hair out of my face, smiling at me then at Kyle. Wow, the happiness coming from him is something that I never thought I'd see. I can't tell you the last time I saw him with a smile that reaches his eyes.

Kyle's hand is still on the small of my back, leading me inside behind my dad. I look around his kitchen. It's clean and the house is a total bachelor pad. We sit down and my dad sets out a huge platter of grilled chicken and a salad.

"Looks great, Dad."

He beams at me happily, and he sits down and starts to fill my plate with way too much food. I laugh, looking at him. "Dad, I think that may be a bit too much."

He shakes his head. "You're carrying my grandbaby, you need to be healthy." With that he adds another bit of salad. Then his smile falls. "If you want me to be a part of her life."

I have thought about this. Should I let him in my life? Should I let him in my baby's? I think I just need to keep my guard up. He was not as horrible as Mom, but he didn't protect me as he should have. That will always be in the back of my mind. "We will see how it plays out, Dad." I smile as nicely as possible.

He nods and smiles at me, cutting up his chicken.

Kyle reaches under the table, his hand curling around my thigh. I lean over and kiss him on the cheek, enjoying this moment.

Life can change in a heartbeat. I wish I could have told myself to have faith, that nothing lasts forever and that one day it will get better.

Once we have finished dinner, we all sit on the front porch together, watching the sun go down. "You have a small slice of heaven here, Dad." He has a huge open field of beautiful green grass.

"I would like to see your place," Dad says.

I look at Kyle and he nods. "Come on, it's right down the road." I motion for Dad to follow us. Kyle keeps a tight grip on my hand as he leads me down the small steps. Kyle has this fear that, at any second, I'm going to fall and the baby will fall out of me. The second part is absolutely ridiculous.

Kyle allows Dad to help me inside the truck, but he never

leaves my side. Kyle doesn't trust my dad, but I think it's because he's very unforgiving when it comes to me because he is so protective.

Dad sits in the back, looking out the window. His place is the first house on the turnoff, but it's not right by the road. "Who all lives in these houses?" Dad asks.

"They all belong to members of the club. We all wanted to be close to each other. So I bought a ton of land, and all the guys started building." I love that. I love that everyone in the club is so close to each other. These guys are badass and they have a dark side, but I've never seen that side of them.

Kyle puts in the code to the gate and it opens, leading down the huge driveway to our house. I look at Kyle, his arms flexing as he drives. My heart is happy. He makes me happy. Every day, life just gets better being around him.

"Wow," Dad whispers behind me. I love that Cassandra is going to be able to grow up in a great environment. Kyle parks and we walk inside the house. I take Dad upstairs to her nursery. The walls are white, and the room is decorated with light pink flowers. Kyle spent hours putting everything together. He went over every detail in the room, making sure it was ready for her.

Dad walks around the room studying everything. I sit down in the rocking chair and hold one of her stuffed animals in my lap. Dad leans against the crib, thinking. "Did you inherit the money?" he asks out of the blue.

"What?" I never expected him to ask that—plus how did he know Joshua was dead? I guess he could have connected the dots.

He looks to the door to make sure no one is there, and he takes a step closer to me and leans in. "Did you get the money?" he asks again, his voice more urgent.

I blink in shock, "Why are you asking that?"

"Your mother is broke, honey," he whispers. "She needs money, and I think once she has that, she will be better again."

It hits me like a ton of bricks. He has betrayed me in the worst way. This was all a ruse for him to get money from me. In the beginning he may have been trying to do the right thing, but now he is here for the wrong reason. He is standing here in my daughter's bedroom, and I will not let it be defiled by this shit.

I'm hurt; all I ever wanted was for my dad to want me and to be a part of my life, but he just wants her. "Is this the only reason you came here in the first place?" I ask, my voice barely above a whisper. His face falls, and I know that he lied to all of us. They fooled us and it cuts deep. "Get out," I say softly.

His eyes widen in shock. "Baby girl, you can't do that. Please try to understand."

"Get out," I demand more loudly. He reaches out and tries to touch my hand, but Kyle stops him.

"You heard her," Kyle growls, twisting my dad's arm behind his back. I hear them fighting all the way out of the house. I stare at the now-empty room, crushed but also feeling foolish because I allowed them to hurt me. My own parents never wanted me except as a pawn to use in their games. Money. That's all they ever saw in me. Now I think my father did have a part in giving me away so they could live a better life.

The door slams loudly. I flinch at the sound and wait for Kyle to come to me. I don't look up from the floor. I'm ashamed because Kyle helped him.

Kyle kisses the back of my head before he sits in front of me. He cups my cheeks. "Angel," he says softly and I look at him—that causes the dam to break. I cry. I cry for the small child that wanted her daddy. The eighteen-year-old girl who was forced to marry a monster to benefit them. They threw me to the wolves, and yet I still had hope.

Kyle holds me and allows me to let go of all the pain and

heartache and to finally grieve the suffering I have been dealt and grieve for the old me that never once had her parents truly want her. I thought my dad was going to change his life, not for me but for himself, although there was no hope for her. But he isn't going to do that. He was here trying to get in my good graces just because of money.

"I am so sorry, baby," Kyle whispers, kissing my forehead. My cheek is pressed against his chest, which is shaking.

I sniff, wiping the tears from my face. "I shouldn't have gotten my hopes up." I sit back in the chair and hold onto the stuffed animal like it's going to keep me grounded. "It's my fault for even entertaining the idea that my dad was going to change his life and want to be a part of mine," I whisper, staring into space.

He shakes harder and cups my face. "You're not to blame for this, don't ever fucking do that. Your dad is a piece of shit." He looks away, his jaw clenched.

I nod. "I know, but it makes me sad. He did this in her room. It makes me feel like he defiled it in a way," I whisper, closing my eyes, sadness overflowing again at the thought of my daughter.

"It doesn't matter, baby. You have me and you have the guys. We are your family. I will always take care of you, no matter what." He rubs my back.

I nod, letting out a deep breath, calming myself. "I feel better now." I smile and Kyle's whole body visibly relaxes. He helps me out of the chair and walks with me downstairs to the living room.

"I think I want some chocolate," I tell Kyle, rubbing my belly. He laughs and we head toward the kitchen. I stop dead in my tracks seeing my mother standing right in the middle of our kitchen with Dad right beside her. I freeze as I see a small pistol in her hand.

Both of them have been digging in my purse, which is on the bar. They look at me and then at Kyle, who picks me up and ducks out of the room. I gasp as the bullet hits the wall where we were standing. She just shot at us!

Kyle runs with me up the stairs into his bedroom, slams the door, and locks it. He pulls up a tablet and presses a button, and a door slides open inside the closet. Kyle takes my hand, dragging me across the room. "You stay in here until I get you or one of the guys comes to get you. I love you, angel." He pushes a button, locking me inside.

"Wait, stay with me!" I yell through the door, which clicks as it locks. A screen on the wall allows me to see all around the house. Kyle is standing in the bedroom, staring at the wall. I touch the screen where he is standing. I'm scared for him.

He closes his eyes for a second and, right before my eyes, his expression fully changes. Gone is the sweet man I know, replaced with the president of the Devil Souls MC.

He walks out of the bedroom, making sure to lock the door behind him as an extra precaution. I hold my stomach, sitting down on the small chair resting in the corner, my eyes glued to the screen. That's when I remember I have my cell phone. I text the guys, letting them know there's trouble.

Kyle

Rage

That is all I feel, seeing both of them digging through her purse, trying to find whatever they can.

It makes me fucking sick. I'm disgusted by both of them. Her dad had me fucking fooled, or maybe I wanted him to be good to her so badly because she wanted it.

Her crying broke my heart into a million little pieces, and I wanted to rip him into shreds. Then seeing her mother waiting in the kitchen and shooting at us?

That just signed their death warrant.

I walk down the stairs, not even bothering to try to hide. I look down at my phone, and I know exactly where they are.

They're hiding in the fucking pantry.

What the fuck do they think that will accomplish? Then I see that they have Chrystal's purse in there with them, trying to salvage whatever they can.

This shit is absolutely ridiculous. I walk over to the pantry, hearing them talking inside. "Look in the side pocket!" her mother hisses. I lock the door so they can't get out. They run into the door, trying to break it down. I laugh and put a chair under the doorknob as an extra precaution. I hear my brothers outside, so I walk to the front door and wait for them to run up the stairs.

"You okay?" Torch asks as he reaches me, his hands flexing, ready for a fight. I shake my head in anger at what the fuck just happened in our house, a place where Chrystal is supposed to feel safe. Now there's a bullet hole in the wall in our kitchen where her own mother tried to hurt her and, worst of all, her father betrayed her.

"I'm fine, I need to get to Chrystal. Take them to the club." I give Torch a pointed look and he nods. "They're in the pantry, locked in."

They laugh and walk into the kitchen, and I make my way upstairs to get Chrystal. I unlock the doors, and she is standing there with tears in her eyes. "Baby," I say softly, and she splits the distance between us and crashes into me. I pick her up and carry her to the bed. "You need to rest, baby." I smooth her hair out of her face. This stress can't be good for her or the baby.

"I know, I'm just shocked at everything that has happened." She closes her eyes, and I run my hand down her side. She's shaking as she rubs her eyes.

"I know, honey, but it's over, and you will never see either of them again." I kiss her forehead. Little by little her breathing evens out as exhaustion takes over. I pull the blanket up to her neck. I take out my phone and text Torch, telling him to deal with it because, at this point, I am way over both of them. I don't care what happens to them as long as they never step foot in her life again.

8

CHRYSTAL

THE NEXT MORNING

I WAKE UP TO PAIN. I groan and look at the clock on the nightstand. It reads 6:00 a.m. and I clench my eyes closed as the contraction ends.

Kyle wakes up and puts his hand on my stomach. "What's the matter?"

I sit up slightly. "I think I just had a contraction." I let out a deep breath, rubbing my stomach, feeling Cassandra kicking.

"Do I need to call the doctor?" He scoots off the bed and walks around to my side.

"I think it's just Braxton Hicks. I'm going to go to the bathroom."

He takes my hand and helps me out of bed, and he helps me into the bathroom. Right before I reach the toilet, a gush of liquid flows down my legs. I eye the floor as a puddle pools around my feet. Kyle pales and I'm freaking out too, because it hits us both that my water just broke.

"I think we need to go to the hospital."

Kyle picks me up and sets me on the toilet, and he runs as fast as he can to the baby's room, grabbing everything that we have packed. I walk into the bedroom and change my clothes and clean up. I'm trying not to think that this could be it. I could be giving birth to my angel soon.

Kyle walks into the bedroom and stops dead in his tracks when he sees me. "Chrystal! Why are you standing there?" he asks and practically lifts me onto the bed.

I laugh, but that's cut short when I have another contraction. "OUCH!" I hiss and rest my head against his stomach. "Fuck, fuck, fuck," Kyle repeats over and over, his whole body stiff, until the contraction ends. Why do I feel like he's going to have a harder time with this than I will?

He rubs my back until I'm ready to move again. "Come on, honey, we need to go to the hospital." He picks me up and carries me outside to the truck then comes back and gets our things.

We sit in silence on the way to the hospital. He holds my hand and constantly kisses the back then the front, trying to soothe me. The nerves are already kicking in, especially once I see the hospital come into view.

I am taken to my room, and the nurse puts monitors on me and starts an IV. I'm shaking as everything around me is a whirlwind. I'm ready to be a mom but, at this moment, I am completely scared. I don't know what could happen and how much pain I am going to experience. There are so many unknowns.

"Alright, sweetheart, relax for me." The nurse pulls up the blanket, and I focus on Kyle.

"The baby was breech at the last doctor's appointment, and we aren't sure if she has turned yet," Kyle tells her. I completely forgot about that.

"You're dilated to a three," the nurse informs me and walks across the room to grab an ultrasound machine.

Please, God, let her be turned, I pray.

Kyle and I both eagerly watch the screen, and a few minutes later the nurse finally speaks. "She is still breech." Oh no. That means that most likely I'm going to have to have a C-section. Kyle kisses my forehead, and I close my eyes as the reality sets in.

Hours later I'm prepped for surgery. Kyle is getting ready too, since he's going to be in there with me. I can't imagine doing this alone.

I'm wheeled into the operation room; then I'm given a spinal tap to numb me from the waist down. I wish I had a huge-ass Xanax right now so I was so doped up that I wouldn't be aware that I'm about to be cut open. The anticipation is what is scaring me.

The door opens and I hold out my hand for Kyle to take as he sits right beside me. They put up a sheet so neither of us can see what's going on.

Kyle rests his forehead against mine, and I put my hand on the back of his head as I hear shuffling all around me. "You may feel some pressure," my doctor tells me, and I tighten my hand on the back of Kyle's head.

"Breathe, angel," he whispers, rubbing my cheekbone.

After what feels like forever, I see the nurses around me move to the end of the bed, and then I hear the most beautiful sound in the world.

My angel. I grin and Kyle laughs with happiness. He stands up as they raise her over the sheet and we get our first glimpse of her. Wow. Before I can really say anything, they take her across the room. Kyle looks torn as to whether to go to her or stay with me. "Go with our daughter." I want her safe. I close my eyes and, for the first time since all of this started this morning, I relax knowing she's safe and that all of this will soon be over.

Holy sore is exactly how I feel. It's around 8:00 p.m., and Cassandra is asleep against my chest. Kyle pulled the bed next to us over so he can lie next to me tonight.

"Are you hurting?" Kyle whispers so he doesn't wake up Cassandra.

I shift in bed to get a little more comfy, my stitches pulling. "I'm just sore right now." I rest my head against his shoulder. He gently rubs Cassandra's small back. We're both so in love with her. I just want to shelter her forever and make sure she is safe from all the awful things in the world.

I stare down into her little face with a mission to make sure that I never fail her, I promise to be there through everything her life throws at her. One thing I know for sure: I am going to give her the childhood she deserves.

"She looks just like you." Kyle smiles, running his fist gently down the side of her face. I rub my eye with the back of my hand, and I wince when something sharp scratches me. I pull my hand back and see a huge-ass ring on my finger. Kyle takes my hand, kissing the back of it. My heart starts racing immediately at the realization of what this means.

"Kyle," I whisper, completely shocked and too scared to say anything.

"Marry me? I want nothing more than for you to carry my name, have more of my babies, and let me love you the way you're supposed to be loved." In one second he puts every single part of my fractured heart back together, and I kiss him because I can't speak yet. I am way too overwhelmed with emotions.

"Well," he mutters against my lips, and I pull back, laughing, which causes my belly to move.

"Ouch." I touch the side of my stomach, waiting for the pain to subside.

"Fuck, be careful, baby." He takes Cassandra from me, holding her close.

"Yes, I will marry you," I finally answer, and he gives me the most beautiful look. I know wholeheartedly that he loves me fully and completely. My dreams have come true. My forever is just now beginning.

EPILOGUE

ONE YEAR LATER

"Kyle, come on. You have to tell me," I beg for the hundredth time since he told me he has a surprise for me.

"Just a few more steps, honey," he urges. We went on a ride while I was blindfolded, so I have no idea where he has taken me. We finally stop walking, and he takes the blindfold off my eyes.

I see a huge building that was just built beside the club; I've been wondering who built it. Then my eyes connect to the sign, "Chrystal's Haven." My nose burns immediately as the tears fill my eyes. "Kyle, did you build this for me?" I ask, trying to hold myself back from crying.

He grips my face, his eyes showing his emotions. This has been a dream of mine, and I wanted to get started on it, but Cassandra has been my sole focus for the last year.

"I wanted to make your dream come true, your safe haven."

I shake my head. "No, Kyle, you're my safe haven. You're the one who made my dreams come true. You."

He grins happily, making my heart sing with happiness. "I love you."

I close my eyes and allow those words to sink deep into my

soul. I open my eyes slowly. "I love you too. We both love you." I cup my stomach, and he looks down in shock.

"You're...?" he asks. I nod and he laughs, picking me up off the ground and swinging me around. I take in the moment, taking in his happiness. He sets me down on the ground, and he gets down on his knees right in front of me and everyone, grinning. "Now who is completing my dreams?" He winks and I laugh, shaking my head. If he only knew how he's the one who makes my world go around.

The end is always just the beginning.

JACK

1

JEAN

WHERE IS THAT FUCKING BASTARD? I look around the parking lot, looking for my boyfriend's car.

That stupid, ignorant leech has been cheating on me. How do I know that, you may ask?

He's getting even suckier in bed than usual—the small effort that he gave is way more lacking and now he's just a three-pump chump when before he was at least six.

So here I am, following him, looking for a reason to leave his ass.

I spot his car towards the back of the lot and I park right next to it. He told me he was going to his mother's. I didn't know his mother worked in a sex shop.

But I guess weirder things have happened. Maybe his dad is a fucking dildo or something. That would make a lot of sense.

I trot my ass up the parking lot, my heart racing, preparing myself for what I'm going to see.

Maybe he's going to be generous and get me a vibrator to make up for his awful effort? That would be fabulous because I could take it and leave his ass.

I pull open the door and my eyes zero in on him instantly.

My eye immediately twitches when I see his lips on a big-tit blonde bimbo that looks like she has been rode hard and put up wet—he isn't responsible for the "rode hard" part, I'm sure.

I walk over to the wall and spot the biggest dildo I can find. Perfect. I smile as I tear it from the wrapper and raise the sucker like I'm a fucking softball pro and his head is the ball.

I walk up behind him and he doesn't even notice. "Ohhhh, Gary boyyy," I sing, and he rips his lips away from her, his eyes so wide I'm afraid they'll hit the ground.

"Caught you, stupid fucker!" I scream as loud as I can because that shit just feels great.

I swing and hit his face as hard as I can. His head snaps back and I laugh because this is comical.

He falls back against at the counter but I don't let up. "You can cheat on me with this trash, you're stupider than I thought!" I screech and hit him over the head. He tries to beat me off (pun not intended).

"You." Whack. "Stupid." Whack. "Ignorant." Whack. "Three." Whack. "Inch." Whack. "Dick." Whack. "Mother." Whack whack. "Fucker!" I scream the last part and hit him one last time right between the legs.

I look at the blonde bimbo who looks shocked and she starts to open her mouth. I point the huge pecker at her, daring her to speak to me. She runs off and I smile because that is the smartest decision her little pea brain ever made.

"Baby, it's not what it looks like!" he begs.

Okay, he is absolutely disgusting. I reach over to the counter and grab a dildo an older gentleman set down there when I entered. It's out of its wrapping—even better.

I wait for the perfect moment for him to speak again and I shove the sucker in his mouth, "Wow, Gary, you have never looked better," I say gleefully. I whack him on the side of his face with the huge pecker again.

I look at the older gentleman and he's pale. "That was my

dildo. I brought it from home to get another one in that size for my ass."

That does it.

I fall to the ground as Gary spits the dildo out of his mouth. I hold my stomach, laughing hard because that just made my day, my year, my whole entire life. "Look, Gary, you have this man's ass juices in your mouth," I wheeze and roll over to my side.

Gary looks at me like he'll murder me, but honestly not one fuck is given in this moment.

A minute later I manage to gather myself. I stand up and put the pecker on the counter, half tempted to bring that sucker home with me because that's even better than a baseball bat.

I look around the sex shop and see everyone's eyeing me like I'm a loon, but if they had dealt with the shit I have dealt with when it comes to this man, they would be acting crazy too.

I throw the dildo on the ground by him and walk out of the door without a backwards glance. I can feel eyes on me but I can't bring myself to care.

I want something different in my life. I've dated losers on top of losers my whole life. It's like a sickness my sisters and I have.

I was a bartender but I got fired because I just have a temper and my mouth tends to outrun my mind. It gets me in a lot of trouble.

But not being myself would be the worst crime.

I get in my car and drive right down the road to the gas station where I currently work.

I don't mind it so much. I love seeing all of the crazy shit people do, so it's not that bad, but it's not what I want to do in life. What I *do* want to do is something I have never been one hundred percent sure about.

2

JEAN

I WALK INSIDE and toss my purse behind the counter, just as a few customers walk into the store—one who doesn't belong here, one who deserves to be plastered on my wall, spread-eagle.

He looks around the store for a second before he turns to look at me. I peek behind me to actually make sure it's me he's looking at.

Maybe god is starting to feel sorry for me for all the shit he has thrown at me? He walks up to the counter, looking better the closer he gets.

He's a biker. I love trouble and it's written all over him. My ovaries are singing at the sight of him.

He tilts his head to the side, studying me, looking me up and down as best as he can.

"Do I know you?" I can't resist the urge to ask.

He smirks. "I just witnessed you beat a man with a dildo, baby."

My face burns. He must have witnessed my mental breakdown. His smile widens. "I also know that you're mine and you're coming with me." He licks his lips, leaning across the counter, his deep, beautiful eyes searching mine intently. "I love crazy and it seems, baby, you're as crazy as it gets."

He lifts his hand for me to take and I look him over once more. Fuck it. "The name is Jean." I grab my purse from under the counter and I can hear my boss yelling as he sees me leaving.

"Fuck you too, Larry!" I yell. I hate that fucker. He always looked at my ass and smelled like grease.

He grins again at that slight glimpse of my crazy, then grips my hand and leads me out of the store straight to a beautiful bike.

I almost come at the sight of him getting on and straddling the beast. My ovaries are full-on screaming in pure delight.

I am so fucked.

"Get on," he demands, turning the bike on the ground that's vibrating under my feet. His arms flex as he revs up the engine.

"Well shit, don't beg, I'll get on," I joke and get on behind him without a second thought.

He laughs and revs the bike again, then reaches back, grabbing my legs and pulling me closer to him.

"Where are we going?" I ask, wrapping my arms around his middle. He grips my leg, pulling me even closer to him.

"To my house, so I can decorate my bed with you." He winks and takes off without me answering him, getting onto the road that will take us straight out of town.

Sounds like a good idea to me.

∼

WE DRIVE AND DRIVE BEFORE HE COMES TO A STOP OUTSIDE OF A beautiful ranch house on the outskirts of Raleigh, Texas. I live three hours from here.

I am certifiably crazy. I don't know this man nor do I even know his name. I left my car in the parking lot of the gas station and didn't tell my family where I was going.

But hey, crazy is my middle name. My father is a police officer and he arrested my mother but he didn't take her to jail. He took her to his house.

Fate is repeating itself, so it's their fault. On my tombstone it better read "Here lies Jean. Her death is because of her parents' crazy genes."

"Nice digs. Where do you plan to bury my remains?" I ask as I slide off of the seat and look around the place. I spot a tree over in the corner of property. I point at it. "That looks like a great place to me."

He just looks at me like I am utterly ridiculous, but he's not wrong to think that. I am. He doesn't respond to me, so I continue to mumble about my death and what will cause it.

Hopefully it's from amazing sex or something along those lines. I would be fully satisfied to die that way.

"I'm not going to kill you," he finally answers and unlocks the front door to his house, pushing it open for me to walk inside.

"Ladies first."

I walk inside, looking around the place. I have to admit it's beautiful and not much of a bachelor pad. It's definitely masculine, though, but in a tasteful way.

I set my purse on the counter but take my phone out, slipping it into my back pocket. "Want to order pizza for dinner?" he asks, setting his keys on the counter.

It's so casual, but I'm not sure how this is supposed to go. "That sounds good to me." I sit down onto the counter and watch him putter around the room.

Now what?

I have no clothes, I quit my job and I beat up my boyfriend with a huge-ass dildo. There is no coming back from that.

He reaches into the fridge, grabbing some beers. "Let's go." He motions towards the back of the house and pulls open the door, and I fall in love.

He has a huge-ass hot tub, an in-ground pool, an enormous fire pit, which is where he is headed, and an outdoor bar area with a pizza oven and grill. It has it all.

He hands me the beer and I sit down beside him, "First off, I'm not going to hurt you. Get that shit out of your head right now."

I laugh, "Well, that's good to know." He shakes his head and takes a long pull of his beer, my eyes moving to his throat, admiring him.

He smiles and shakes his head. "My name is Jackson. I'm a member of the Devil Souls MC." He really is a bad boy. I knew that the second he strutted into the gas station and told me I was his.

No one else would have the balls to do that.

"So, Jack, you witnessed my mental breakdown first hand." I scoot farther in the seat and tuck my legs under my body.

He full-on laughs, making him look younger. "I sure did. I was driving past and happened to see you beating a guy over the head with it"

I laugh loudly—the sight that must have made. "I caught him cheating. I do think he deserved it." I shrug my shoulders but I won't lie and say it didn't hurt.

"I can go back and kill him if you want?" Jackson asks, looking all serious. Ehh, I don't think I want to do that. "Rain check on that?" I wink and he looks kind of sad at the fact.

At least I'm not the only crazy one here.

"I should have kept it for emergencies." I sigh dramatically and lean back in my seat.

"I will buy you all the toys you want," Jackson informs me, and I laugh loudly because that is such a man response.

I eye him up and down. "I guess you're going to make me a kept woman too?" I tease.

He lifts his beer, pointing at me. "That's the whole point, angel." He licks his lips before taking a drink of his beer.

I blink once, twice, three times, shocked that those words came out of his mouth. "Tell me more."

He turns around in his seat, facing me. "Going to marry your ass, plant some babies in you and live happily ever after."

I snort. "Shit, you're crazy." I cackle harder the longer I think about what he's suggesting. Like it's going to work like that.

He leans over, putting his hand gently on my face. "Normal is overrated. The best things in life are wild, crazy and come completely by surprise." His thumb strokes my cheek and he leaves me sitting to walk inside the house.

Well shit, for the first time in my life I'm speechless.

What did I get myself into?

I eye his ass through the window. Never mind. I remember.

3

JEAN

I've two missed calls from my sister and one from my mom. I guess they just probably discovered I skipped town. My phone buzzes again and it's my father. Well, I can't ignore him. "Hello," I say cheerfully.

"Jeanette Lynn Ambrose, where the fuck have you been? I found your vehicle at your work and they said you ran off with a biker," my dad yells through the phone, and Jack's head snaps in my direction, hearing my dad bitching me out.

"Well it's true," I say simply, totally unfazed. My dad is a bad motherfucker and everyone I know is pretty much scared of him. Not me though.

"Fuck me! Tell me where you are so I can kick his ass." He sighs and I hear a thumping sound like he's banging his head against the wall.

"Hey, Jackson. Dad wants our address. He said he wants to come and kick your ass."

"Jeanette, he could be crazy! Do you want to die?"

I put the phone on speaker. "Well I don't particularly want to die," I drag out, and Jack chuckles under his breath. "The address is…" Jack rattles it off loud enough so my dad can hear.

"Shit, are you telling me you ran off with a Devil?" my dad says after a moment of silence.

I look at Jackson and he looks at the phone, his face set as he prepares for my dad to say what he needs to say.

"Yeah," I mumble.

My dad cusses under his breath. "Wait, Jackson?"

My head snaps back. I'm not sure how I didn't even break it and Jackson does the same thing, confused.

"Uhh, Dad, how did you know that?"

"Did you tell him your whole name, baby girl?" Dad asks the both of us.

Jackson arches an eyebrow, waiting for me to tell him. "Jeanette Lynn Ambrose."

He busts out laughing, shocking me, and my dad joins in, leaving me totally confused as to what is happening.

What's the big joke here?

"Well at least you're safe," my dad says when he finally composes himself. "I'm still going to kick your ass for taking my girl. Watch yourself, Jackson." My dad hangs up, leaving me and Jack alone.

"I was actually at the police station to see your dad. There's been a trafficking issue in the area and we noticed that some girls have gone missing from your town. Our president sent me to talk to your dad to get his info."

Oh wow, I didn't expect that whatsoever. If this is fate or some shit, then I don't know what is. He just happened to come back from seeing my dad, watched me beat up someone with a dildo and then I hopped on the back of his bike.

Weird, but I'll take it.

"Small world."

Jackson smiles sweetly. "Definitely, sweetheart."

I'm kind of on my toes around him because I don't know him, but my dad trusting him is huge, so that makes me feel better.

"Sorry about my dad wanting to beat your ass."

He scoots over until he's right next to me, sliding the pizza and drinks along with him on the coffee table.

"I would be disappointed if he didn't. Then that would mean I'd have to kick his ass for not caring."

What's up with these men being violent? "Did anyone ever tell you that there are easier ways to settle things than being violent?" I tease.

He rolls his eyes so hard I'm surprised that they don't get stuck in his skull. "Says the girl who chose a fucking big-ass dildo to beat up her ex."

Okay, maybe I was being a bit dramatic there.

"Touché, baby cakes."

"Here's some pizza." He hands me a piece and drink. I bet he's trying to stop me from talking, but I'll let it slide since he's feeding me.

"Since you plan on impregnating me and making me wifey, we have to have nicknames for each other," I tease, and he doesn't say a word. His eyes are fixed on the TV, ignoring me.

Well huh.

I can't help but admire him once again. He truly is beautiful, the way the tattoos look against his tan skin, his beautiful green eyes and his dark brown hair that's messed up from riding the bike. Him being a biker just takes the cake as far as I'm concerned.

I notice that he has put in a scary movie. I'm a huge wimp when it comes to those kinds of movies.

Is it weird that I'm deathly afraid of being possessed? I've had nightmares of that and being pulled down the hallway into the pits of hell.

I hurry and eat my pizza before it gets to the really scary part. "What movie is this?" I try to ask calmly.

"*The Conjuring.*"

Yeah, I am so done for.

I wipe my hands on the napkin and scoot farther up on the couch in case something tries to crawl out from under the couch and snatch me.

I bite my thumbnail, scooting a little closer to Jackson as the mother goes into the basement and the light isn't on.

She lights a match and then hands shoot out of the dark, clapping, making the match go out.

I scream like a banshee, clinging to Jackson like I'm dying. "Oh god, my heart," I moan and rest my head on his shoulder blade. He looks shocked.

"Shit, I didn't know that would scare you so bad," he says in a gentle voice. He turns off the TV and I try to breathe again.

Call me a pussy, I don't care. I can't handle those kinds of movies. "Why didn't you tell me?" he asks softly, pushing my hair out of my face so he can see me.

"I don't know," I mumble. My guard is totally down.

He gathers me up in his arms and onto his lap. I rest my head in the crook of his neck and just allow him to hold me.

No one has ever just held me because I felt scared. I rest my hand on his warm chest. "Thank you for caring," I whisper.

"Fuck, I don't want you scared ever. I don't give a fuck if it's a movie or not."

There goes my heart right out of the window. I don't respond but I just cuddle deeper into his chest, loving this very moment. God, he smells so nice.

It's around ten o'clock at night at this point. He moves a bit, then a blanket comes into view as he covers me up like I'm a baby.

"Are you swaddling me?" I joke and wrap my arm around his neck, feeling his pulse with my fingers.

"Yes," he chuckles and rests his head on top of mine.

Music slowly drifts around the room. I close my eyes, enjoying the moment fully. "I guess I'm kind of glad that I hopped on the back of your bike, Jacky-poo."

"Oh god, I guess I'm happy I picked your ass up too," he laughs, his body vibrating under mine.

"I knew you liked me," I sigh, my body getting heavy as I fight sleep.

He smooths my hair back, running his fingers along the strands. "I do, baby." My heart swells at his sweet words.

His fingers work magic, lulling me to sleep.

Jean

The light streaming through the room wakes me up. It takes me a second to understand where I am.

Jackson is still asleep right next to me. Both of us slept on the couch all night long. I look at the clock on the wall and it reads six a.m. Hell no, I am not getting up this hour.

"You want to lay down upstairs?" Jackson says suddenly, scaring the piss out of me.

"Yeah, if you want." I sit up and climb off the couch, the cold air hitting me and causing goosebumps to break out across my skin.

He notices and wraps the blankets around my shoulders before taking my hand. "Come on." His voice is deeper than usual with sleep. That rasp is so sexy.

The upstairs is just as beautiful as the downstairs. He leads me to the back of the house to a huge master bedroom. He pulls back the blankets on the bed and I let the throw blanket hit the floor and crawl in.

He slides in behind me and wraps his arm around my middle, pulling me all the way against his front.

"You're a way good cuddler." I close my eyes, getting warmer by the second. His hand comes up and intertwines our fingers. I smile, loving the sight of our hands together.

"That's not the only thing I'm good at." I can feel his mouth moving up into a grin where it's resting against my shoulder.

I shake my head slightly, close my eyes, and go to sleep.

4

JEAN

After Jackson and I finish breakfast, he says, "Come on, let's go get you some clothes and shit" and grabs his keys off the counter.

I honestly didn't even think about clothes before this. "We can just drive back and get mine?" I offer, since I really don't want to pay for a lot of new stuff as I'm pretty much jobless now.

"We can, but we have a barbecue to go to tonight at the club. I'm paying for it all, so enjoy it, baby doll." He winks and waits at the door for me.

"You don't have to do that." I get off of the couch. "I don't want you to spend all of that money on me," I confess, feeling guilty.

He grips my chin softly. "Hey, none of that sad shit. You're too beautiful to be frowning." Butterflies swarm my belly at him being so sweet to me. I can't resist the urge to wrap my arms around his middle, hugging him.

He hugs me back, his lips kissing me softly on top of my head. Why do I feel so at ease with him? It's like I've always known him in a weird way.

It's not about him buying me clothes. It's him being thoughtful enough to even think of me and my needs, to be sweet to me without even trying to jump into my pants, which is honestly what I thought was going to happen the second I got here.

It wasn't like anything I expected. None of this has been.

I reluctantly let him go but he doesn't let me go far, taking my hand and leading me to the side of the house, where the garage is located.

I hear a vehicle outside of the gate and I look over just as a car whizzes by. "Am I crazy or was that my ex-boyfriend driving past?" I laugh nervously. That car had the same bumper sticker on it that Gary's car has.

"What the fuck?" Jackson cusses and puts me in the truck before he walks down the drive to make sure he's gone.

That's really weird.

Jackson stands there for another minute before he gets in the truck and takes out his phone. "Techy, check my gate camera for the last half an hour and send it to me."

I rub my legs, trying to calm my nerves. I'm not afraid of Gary, that's for sure, but I am kind of creeped out that it could have been him.

He would have had to follow us from three hours away. I can see why he would be mad since I kind of humiliated him, but he humiliated me too, so in my eyes it was fair.

So I do what every girl does when she needs something. I call my dad and put my phone on speaker for the both of us to hear.

"Hey, baby girl," he answers, and I grin. My dad has always been my best friend.

"Can you do me a favor? Can you check to see if Gary is still in town because I'm pretty sure I saw him right by Jackson's house," I tell him, and Jackson grips the stirring wheel hard, his jaw set.

JACK

"What the fuck? I forgot that guy even existed. When did you even break up with him?" Jackson looks over at me, his face red, trying not to laugh. How do I explain that to my dad?

"Well, I caught him cheating yesterday. I beat him up with a three-foot dildo and hopped on the back of Jackson's bike. That pretty much sums it up."

Jackson thumps his head against the window at my blunt honesty. "What the fuck, Jeanette?" My dad trails off before sighing. "I'll go check." He hangs up the phone.

I laugh to myself because I can just picture my dad rubbing his face in annoyance. It can't be helped. Me, Mom and my sister are almost exactly the same—no hiding how we are.

"Do you have any siblings?" I ask Jackson once he pulls into town, I love that he lives right outside of town but you wouldn't know it. It's in a beautiful gated community but the houses are spread out far enough you wouldn't even notice.

I can't help but admire him, the way his arms flex as he turns the wheel, how relaxed he is in the seat, the way his thick thighs are straining against his jeans.

I just know under that shirt he's wearing he has abs that are made for licking and kissing.

"I don't. My mom and dad had me late in life. They passed away a few years ago." I can see the sadness on his face thinking about them.

My heart hurts. I reach over and take ahold of his hand. "I'm sorry for your loss. I will share my parents with you, but I've got to admit, my mother is an exact clone of me."

He laughs, his eyes lightening. "Two of you. However could I survive?" he teases.

"Actually three of me; my sister is included in that." I giggle at his horrified expression.

"Your poor dad," he whispers, and I reach over, smacking him slightly on the shoulder. "My dad is perfectly happy with his life, thank you very much."

Jack's face turns serious. "I have no doubt about that, baby doll."

Well, there goes my poor battered heart out of the window once again. How does he always know the correct things to say?

Jack

I don't like the fact that she thinks she saw her ex, and I have a gut feeling that it was him. If he followed her here, then he's not up to anything fucking good.

I keep a close eye on her as she shops. Like I could keep my fucking eyes off of her in the first place.

She is so effortlessly beautiful, the way she talks, the way she moves from rack to rack of clothes is mesmerizing in itself.

"Can I help you?" one of the workers in the shop asks.

"Just waiting on her." I nod my head in the direction of Jean, who is holding up a pair of jeans.

"Her?" she says snottily.

I glare at her. "What the fuck is that supposed to mean?" I snap. I don't like that disrespectful shit and especially in my face. Woman or not, I will put you in your place, hands down.

She backs away, her face paling by the second before she runs off to the front of the building.

I turn around, coming face to face with Jean, who is grinning like the fucking Grinch. "What's the goofy-ass grin on your face?"

"You stood up for me. If you're trying to get in my pants, then it's totally working." She licks her lips, looking me up and down, causing my dick to harden under her gaze almost instantly.

It was fucking hard to sleep next to her all night long and not taste her pussy. I am aching for it.

She leaves me wanting, going back to her shopping. I'll buy

her whatever the fuck she wants as long as I get to have her, all of her.

"Sir." I turn my head and come face to face with a mall cop. "One of the ladies here in the shop told me you harassed her. I am going to have to escort you from the building."

What do I do?

I laugh in his fucking face. "You need to tell that bitch that lying will get her ass in trouble." I look directly as her huddling behind the counter. "She wasn't afraid a second ago when she was trying to hit on me."

"Ohhhhh, she was what?" I hear Jean say dramatically. I grin because I just heard the voice I heard just yesterday when her fucking ex was getting his shit handed to him.

She dashes right past me, throwing me her clothes in the process. I catch them and sit back to watch the show.

"Listen here, you little prissy, bitchy, tattletale, hippo-looking ass! What gives you the right to start trouble because someone wasn't falling for your nastiness?" She shakes her head all around, waving her hand dramatically.

I try not to laugh because her choice of words is killing me. "Now you need to tell this mall cop person that you lied, 'kay? Or I will stick this high heel point straight up your nostril and into your brain!" She waves the shoes towards her face.

I cover my mouth and everyone else is looking shocked that this is happening, I know without a doubt that she will follow through with her threat.

"Ma'am, you need to leave." The mall cop starts to reach for her arm.

"Touch her and die." I glare at him, stepping up between them. "I dare you," I growl, and he takes a step back. "Come on, doll, let's go to another shop."

Jean eyes the girl and then the mall cop. "You're lucky I'm in a good mood today. You don't want to see the bad side of me."

She finally smiles and tosses the shoe towards the sales lady, then takes my hand.

"I'm kind of hungry. Shall we get food?" she says cheerfully like none of this happened.

"Yeah, let's go feed you, honey." I rub her hand and she pushes her hair over her shoulder, everything totally forgotten.

5

JEAN

WE SHOPPED UNTIL WE DROPPED, but right now I'm getting ready with my new things since we're going to his club tonight for a party.

It would be a lie if I said I wasn't nervous to meet his people. I know that his brothers in the MC mean a lot to him because he talks about them all of the time…well, since I met him yesterday.

I've been texting my family on and off all day long, my sister and mother both grilling me about Jackson.

My dad calls me. "Hey, baby girl, Gary is nowhere to be seen and his neighbors haven't seen him since yesterday when he came out carrying a bag and left."

Oh no, I probably did see him then

"Okay, thanks, Dad," I mumble, thinking of what he could be up to. I didn't date him long, maybe like a month? I'm not even sure. I think I just didn't want to be alone so I settled and that's something I should have never done.

"Bring the phone to Jackson, okay? I need to speak to him about the case."

"Okay, love you, Daddy."

"Love you, baby."

I stick my head out of the doorway and yell, "Jackson, Dad is on the phone wanting to speak to you!" He comes and takes the phone from me and I go back to my makeup.

Jackson

"Yeah?" I say into the phone.

"The fucker dipped out of town. I think he followed Jeanette. I looked up his record. The fucker has a bunch of restraining orders against him from five different women, and two of them are missing. Connect the dots. He is dangerous."

I knew I had a bad feeling about this. The second she said she saw his car I knew it was him. "Fuck," I grind out between my teeth. The thought of this fucker wanting to harm her drives me ballistic.

"Do you want me to come get her?" her dad offers.

"Fuck no, I will protect her. You know I will." My voice leaves no arguments. I won't allow him to take her, because I will protect what's mine. There's no doubt about that.

"Shit, protect my baby. If I didn't think that was true, I would have already been there." he huffs and hangs up the phone before I can respond.

I look in the bathroom at Jean straightening her hair in front of the mirror. I insisted on buying straighteners for her. I don't plan on sending her ass back home, ever.

I wouldn't let anyone hurt her—that would be their worst nightmare.

A deadly mistake.

Jean

I feel like Jack knows more than me about what is going on

with my ex, but I will be naïve and blissfully dumb because I don't want to worry about it.

I step out of the bathroom dressed in my tight black skinny jeans, with rips in random places and cuffed ends, and booties. My tight olive-green shirt is tucked in, showing off my curves.

Jackson slowly turns to look at me, his eyes heated as he scans me up and down. I love that look on him and knowing that I put it there.

I can't resist the urge to spin in a circle so he'll get the full effect.

"You like what you see, darlin'?" I tease, cocking my hip to the side.

He licks his lips seductively. "Love what I fucking see."

Well damn, I love that response. He walks to me. I don't move, I don't breathe, I just wait to see what he does next.

His hand drifts up my arm, fingers trailing. "You are the most beautiful thing I have ever laid my eyes on."

My eyes burn and I reach out to grip his shirt in my hands, just needing to touch him some way.

"I'm going to kiss you."

"Yes please," I whisper breathlessly.

He ducks his head and I stand on my tippy toes, wrapping my arms around his neck, and our lips meet in a fever of emotions.

Full of passion, full of want and so much more.

It's like for the first time in my life, I'm coming home.

His lips move over mine in a way that can't be explained in words. It's the kind of kiss that will stay with me forever and nothing will ever compare. Nothing will ever compare to him.

He is claiming me, all of me.

I want it all.

I want everything he will give me.

His hands move, cupping my face fully, holding me tenderly.

He slowly pulls away and looks at me, his eyes staring deep into mine.

"That was your last first kiss," he says, completely serious.

I believe him.

I would be lying if I said I didn't think that this is special. Even if he isn't meant to be in my life forever, he was meant to be in my life.

"Okay," I whisper. He smiles sweetly, ducking his head to kiss me once more on my forehead.

Forehead kisses mean so much more. They promise respect and safety. Right now in his arms, I feel so safe and cared for.

"Ready?" He pushes my hair over my shoulder, his fingers drifting softly over my skin and coming to rest at the back of my neck.

More than ready, I think in my head, but I reply, "Yeah, honey."

His nose flares at me calling him that. I have to admit that I love that I affect him deeply with just a few simple words.

He locks the door behind him and we walk to his bike parked in front of the house. I loved riding on the back of his bike with him.

I loved seeing all of the women stopping dead in their tracks at the sight of him. He is pure perfection and right now he is all mine.

He slides on, his jeans cupping his ass tightly and showing off the most glorious bubble butt. "Has anyone ever told you that you could bounce a dime off your ass?"

His shoulders shake as he laughs silently. Then he licks his lips and tries to be serious. "I can't say that anyone has ever told me that."

I take his hand and allow him to help me slide in behind him. My hands drift down his sides to the top of his buns, squeezing slightly. "Now you know," I purr in his ears.

"You're fucking trouble. Better be careful, baby. You're

playing with fire." His hands reach back, wrapping around my thighs and pulling me to him hard, my front flush against his back, my pussy pressed against his butt.

And he says I'm trouble.

He starts the bike and it vibrates under me. I try not to cry out. My hoo-ha is sensitive right now because she's demanding some of Jackson.

Jackson tilts his head back, "Enjoy the ride, baby." He winks and revs up the bike, causing my pussy to tighten.

Oh fuck.

He starts down the driveway, and I lay my head against the small of his back and pray that I don't orgasm on the back of this bike.

The main gate opens and he takes off on the main highway. I shake as I try to hold onto him and enjoy the sensations.

Closer and closer.

All of a sudden he pulls off of the highway and moves behind a building, away from everything.

"What are you doing?" I ask once he shuts off the bike.

"Get your ass off of the bike and take off your pants, now," he demands, his powerful thighs gripping the bike as I slide off.

I shake as I do as I'm told, half needy and half nervous as to what he is doing.

I watch him watching me as I slowly take off my pants and panties in one swoop, leaving me completely naked.

He reaches out and takes my hand, pulling me to him, picking me up as he scoots down the bike.

I'm facing him on the bike, straddling him.

He smiles and my stomach twists as I wonder what he's going to do.

"Lean back." He motions for me to recline across the handle bars. He grips my legs, lifting me up and throwing them over his shoulders.

"I'm starving," he growls, letting out a deep breath across my dripping folds, and I grip onto anything to hold me down.

"Hands under your ass. Don't move unless you want me to stop," he demands, his lips turned up slightly in the knowledge he has me cornered.

No way in hell would I move. I am completely at his mercy.

His tongue moves across my folds, teasing me. "You're fucking soaked," he moans, before he spreads my lips with his fingers, his mouth closing around my clit, sucking hard.

My legs shake instantly. I look at him as he eats me like a man starved and I am his only meal.

"This pussy is mine. All of you is mine," he claims, sneaking two fingers inside of my pussy and curling them as his tongue moves over my clit rapidly.

"Ahh!" I scream, clenching hard on his fingers and coming hard, my whole body shaking, but he doesn't stop.

He keeps on and on until I come once more, not even able to control my body. Me being still completely out of the window, I grip his head and pull his hair as I orgasm once again.

"Hmmm." He smirks before licking my thighs. "Best fucking thing I've tasted. I think I need you for every meal." His tongue glides over his glistening lips.

I just fell in love with this man.

"Let me take care of you." I move on wobbling legs off of the bike, putting on my clothes as best as I can.

"Not on your fucking knees, baby." He stands up and sits me down on his bike, leaving me perfectly level with him.

I slowly unbutton his pants and slide the zipper down, teasing him like he did me in the beginning.

He just fixes heated eyes on me as I grip his pants and pull them down to his thighs.

He isn't wearing any underwear.

I grip him in my hand. "If I knew you were packing like this, I would have jumped you yesterday."

Jackson is big all over. His dick is long and thick, made for pleasuring a woman. He grips the handle bar with his left hand, and I bend over and take him in my mouth, licking the top like it's my favorite sucker.

My eyes don't leave his. I love seeing him come undone from my mouth. I take him as deep as I can, trailing my tongue down as I go.

"Fuck, doll," he grunts when he touches the back of my throat. I repeat the process again and again, slowly torturing him, dragging out his pleasure over and over.

"Take what you need from me, Jackson," I whisper. I know it's killing him to allow me to have control.

His eyes darken and his fingers twist in my hair, enough to pull but not to hurt.

He would never intentionally hurt me.

I relax my throat and grip the base of his dick, moving my hand with each thrust he makes. He fucks my face and my eyes water as I gag the deeper and deeper he moves.

I love every single second of it.

His movements get more erratic the closer he gets to coming, and I move my hand away. His hand moves to my throat, and I watch the very last seconds as he comes undone, his legs shaking, his hand trembling against my throat.

He starts to pull out of my mouth…no, he's coming in my mouth. I grip his ass cheeks, not allowing him to leave, and he comes hard.

"Fuck!" he yells out and stops moving. I swallow every single drop and run my finger across my lips to catch any that slipped out.

Jack wrenches me off the bike and kisses me with so much passion my toes curl. I love that he doesn't care that I probably have his cum on my mouth.

"Time for the party." We both get back on the bike, this time less gracefully than the first time, both of us weak-kneed.

We are only a few minutes from the clubhouse, and it's not what I expected. It's a huge-ass warehouse.

Bikes are littered everywhere with people standing around with cuts and women wearing their own—my guess is they're ole ladies. I learned enough from *Sons Of Anarchy* to not be totally clueless, but I won't tell Jackson that because I think real bikers tend to hate that show.

He parks his bike next to some others at the front of the warehouse. He shuts off the engine and turns to look at me. "Listen, angel, stay by my side or one of the guys in my club at all times, okay?"

I nod without hesitation. I may be irrational sometimes, but I'm not stupid. I intertwine our fingers. "Got it."

He kisses my cheek before moving to whisper something my ear, "I can still taste you on my lips."

I shiver all the way down to my feet. I can't even respond to that. He notices, and I can see the smugness.

"This is the yearly meet of all of the local motorcycle clubs. Some of these guys here are not good, baby, but there's also random nomads that try to start shit." I can see that he's on alert.

"I promise I won't leave you." I grip his hand tighter.

"Now let's have a good fucking time."

I notice that across the lot next to the huge-ass fire are others from his club. I recognize the cut. Along the way, Jackson greets others and I smile politely.

From the corner of my eye I notice some weird random guys standing by themselves, watching the both of us.

"Jackson, why are some of the guys angry when they look at you?" I can't help but ask. I'm on edge, not for my sake but for Jackson's.

Did I mention that I have a protective steak a mile wide? I can't promise you if someone tries to fuck with him that I will sit back twiddling my thumbs.

He pulls me away from everyone. "Some of the guys here are prospects that never made it. They're pissed about it."

That makes sense. I look over my shoulder to see if that weird guy with the bald head is still eyeballing us. He tilts his head to the side, catching me.

Yep, I guess that confirms it.

Jackson moves, blocking the man's eyes from me by having me walk slightly in front of him. I love how protective he is. That shit gets me going every time.

"Jean, this is my President, Kyle." Jackson introduces me to a man who is larger than life. I knew right off the bat when I saw him that he's the leader because he has this air around him that demands attention and respect.

"It's nice to meet you." I shake his hand and he smiles politely, then looks to the woman standing beside him.

"This is my wife, Chrystal," Kyle introduces me to his wife, and she is beautiful. She has kind eyes. She must be protected all costs—she is the kind of woman that has too good of a soul.

"It's really nice to meet you," I tell her truthfully.

She smiles happily and it's clear she can tell I'm genuine. She splits the distance and hugs me. "It's nice to meet you too, honey."

I look at Kyle, who is watching the both of us. I can tell he's pleased. I want to make a good impression because they all mean so much to Jackson.

Next I'm introduced to Ryan, who is a quiet guy just watching everything and everyone.

Jackson's hand is gripping my hip tightly, protectively, as he talks to the guys and I talk to the girls

I'm slowly introduced to Torch, Techy and Butcher, who I find kind of scary. Another MC club I have noticed that the guys are close to is the Grim Sinners MC. I noticed right off the bat that their demeanor is close to the Devils.

I'm a people watcher when I'm not running my mouth and I

know most of the other clubs are intimidated. They stay away as much as possible. They mingle, but they do it and leave.

But I also see the anger, the jealousy and the bitterness.

Especially from that one bald guy who has a stick so far up his ass I'm not sure how he's even moving.

Torch is standing next to me with Jackson on the other side. Torch and I both have been sneaking glances at the weirdo.

I feel someone moving up behind me and I look over to see the bald-headed guy standing around ten feet away. I turn around quickly and pretend to laugh with Chrystal.

Either I'm super paranoid or shit is about to go down. I put my drink down onto the small table in front of me and Jackson's hand tightens on me.

"Do you notice?" I say so softly it's barely a whisper.

"Yeah, baby, I've seen it all night. I'm just not as obvious as you and Torch," he chuckles.

Torch and I both pretend to be offended, "We can't help it if we're nosey," Torch laughs, and Jackson kisses my temple and then he stumbles into me hard, almost knocking me down.

I look at Jackson in shock and see a rock in his hand. Did someone try to throw that at us? That's when I see the bald fucker standing right behind me holding another rock in his hand.

My stomach in twists in knots.

Jackson moves to stand in front of me and the guys all swarm around us. Chrystal grips my hand tightly, pulling us back into the fray of men.

"Did you just try to fucking hit my woman with a rock?" Jackson says in a voice that I don't even recognize as his.

My heart starts pounding in my chest as everything is happening around me like I'm having an out-of-body experience.

"I saw him throw it," Chrystal speaks up, and Kyle looks at

her, heated, then back at the guy. I can feel the air around me changing as the guys get more and more pissed off.

"Tell your bitch to keep her eyes to herself," the bald guy says in a nasty tone, glaring at me like I'm the cause of his problem.

Okay, that pisses me right the fuck off.

Jackson freezes, his hand shaking in mine.

I look at him full on, not even scared of the fucker. He's a pussy. "In case you forgot, I was not the only one looking at you, but your tiny penis only allows you to pick on someone smaller than you to make yourself feel better." I look down at his package, smirking.

Everyone starts laughing, and I mean everyone, Jackson included.

I watch as he rears his hand back and throws another rock. This time everyone witnesses it hurtling straight at me.

It all happens in slow motion as Jack deflects it before it can hit me and it thumps to the ground.

"You just signed your death warrant," Jackson says in the deafening silence that follows.

Before I can retaliate, breathe or blink, Jackson is in front of him, gripping him by the throat and slamming him onto the ground. He hits him over and over in the face, and the only sound I can hear is that of his fists.

I don't hear anyone breathing.

Hours could have passed, it's all blur as Jackson unleashes his inner beast on this guy who tried to hurt me.

I stare at what's left of his face. It's completely mangled, skin hanging off, blood coming out of every hole.

"Jackson," I call out, feeling really sick to my stomach all of a sudden. I don't want him to go to jail for murder. This fucker is not worth it.

He stops and looks at me, his eyes wide with fury. It's so thick I can taste it. He stops hitting him, looking disgusted at even the thought of touching him.

He lets go of his shirt and lets him fall to the ground with a thump, his head rolling to the side...or what's left of it. I'm not sure if he's even breathing, I wouldn't be surprised if Jackson didn't bash in his skull.

Jackson comes to me and slowly the chatter starts up around us. Everyone goes back to their business like none of this happened.

I don't think I could forget it any time soon.

I just want to touch him. The second he's close enough, I wrap my arms around his middle, hugging him tightly.

He protected me. I've never had that in my life besides my dad, but this is different. He wraps his arms around me. "You ready to go home?" he asks, and I nod. I am so ready to get out of here.

"Thank you for protecting me." I grip the front of his shirt, kissing him right in the open in front of everyone.

He grips the back of my head, kissing me back hard. This is his way of claiming me in front of everyone.

"He's lucky I don't finish the job." He starts to get angry again.

"Let's just go home?" I ask. I want to get out of here and just cuddle up to him. He tucks me close into his side and we wave to the others, walking to the bike.

Jean

Once we're back home, I pull him upstairs to his bedroom and straight into the bathroom. I noticed riding home that his knuckles are busted up.

I turn on the shower. I want to get the blood off of him and I just need the heat to make me feel.

I know that I'm loud and obnoxious, but I also feel deeply and I don't want to admit that I'm shaken by what happened.

How could someone just lash out in such a way for really no apparent reason? That floors me.

I pull off my clothes, taking Jackson's with me. He watches my every move, and I can tell that he's concerned for me.

"Shower with me?" I ask, tugging on his hand.

He doesn't answer but he picks me up off the ground, my legs instinctually going around his waist. His hands cup my ass, squeezing slightly.

"I'm going to bite this ass later." He wiggles his eyebrows.

He walks under the spray and the water runs down my back. I close my eyes, tilting my head back, wetting my hair.

"Are you okay, baby?" he asks. I can hear the worry in his voice.

I wipe the water out of my face with my hands. "I'm fine, honey. I'm just confused to what his deal was with me especially. Torch was looking just as much as I was..." I trail off, thinking.

"He's a pathetic piece of shit. It takes a stupid fucker to even dare to speak to a Devils woman like that. Trust me, he is being handled." A sinister smile slides over his face.

I really don't want to know.

I think about the amazing time we had before we got to the clubhouse. I will never be able to look at a bike again without thinking of what we did on his.

"How's your hand?" I wiggle for him to put me down, taking his hand in mine and letting the water run over it.

His knuckles are cracked. I run my finger over the cuts slightly. "I'm sorry, baby. Do they hurt?"

"No, not my first rodeo, sweetheart. No sadness for me, okay?" He tugs on my chin slightly.

"Got it. Now turn around so I can get a full glimpse of that ass." I make a spinning motion with my hand and he slowly turns around for me.

I moan loudly. "It's even better than I imagined, dear god." I cover my face dramatically and he laughs.

"Quit fucking with me." He smacks my ass hard in retaliation.

"Ouch!" I screech with laughter. I wasn't expecting that. My pussy, on the other hand? Loves it.

"Come just shake for me a little bit!" I pinch my fingers together and he glares at me before he attacks.

I laugh loudly at him tickling my sides. "Stop, stop, I'll be good!" I scream as the tears roll down my face from laughing so hard.

He lets me go and I eye him suspiciously, "You are a menace!" I wag my finger at him, but you couldn't take the smile off of my face even if you tried.

I'm happy.

He came into my life when I least expected it. I kind of hit the lowest I could go in my life, but he just turned everything upside down.

And now?

I can't imagine my life without him in it. I know that sounds crazy as I just met him, but I don't think it's how long you know someone, it's the way they make you feel.

My connection to him is a different one.

Looking at him, the water dripping down his body down to his hands that he hurt defending me, I think to myself, holy shit. This is really happening. Whatever this is between us is real and it's happening.

We don't speak during the rest of the shower. We wash each other's bodies with care. It's the most intimate thing I have ever experienced.

We don't bother getting dressed and we crawl into bed together. Jackson moves in between my legs, already hard and pressing against my clit.

He kisses me, carefully, so tenderly, but it's full of so many feelings. My fingers trail up his back, burying in his hair as the kiss gets more heated.

I can't resist the urge to tilt my hips, letting his dick rub over my clit. "Is my baby hungry for me?" Jack whispers against my lips, pushing my hair out of my face and cupping my neck.

"Yes," I moan.

He grips my face, tilting it to the side so he can kiss my neck, licking, sucking gently as he makes his way to the other side.

"Let me see how wet you are for me." His hand snakes in between our bodies, and my whole body jolts the second his finger barely grazes my clit.

"Soaked," his voice rasps, his teeth nipping the side of my neck.

"Only for you." I feed his need to own me.

"That's fucking right, baby, this pussy is mine and mine alone," he growls, pressing his thumb against my clit.

"Fuck, Jack," I grit between my teeth. I'm still sensitive from the many orgasms he gave me earlier.

"You want my dick? Is that what you need?" he demands an answer, tugging on my earlobe with his teeth.

"Please, Jackson," I beg and I'm not ashamed to do it.

He reaches over into the night stand and takes out a condom, rolling it down his dick. I need him so bad, my whole entire body is shaking with it.

He presses the head against my entrance, teasing me, and I want to cry with frustration. He grips both of my hands and throws them above my head, holding me down with one arm.

"Mine," he says slowly as he finally sinks inside.

"Jackson," I hiss. He's much larger than anyone I have been with. The sting of him stretching me is there, but it's just fueling my pleasure.

"Yours," I agree.

He lets me adjust for a few seconds before he's pounding

into me. I can't move, I can't breathe, I am overwhelmed with the pleasure.

Both of us are overtaken by it.

I tilt my hips, wanting more and more.

Both of us are slick with sweat and he moves harder, faster, until everything around me freezes. I dig my nails into his back and come harder than I thought possible.

My whole entire body jerks from the tremors, my pussy clenching down on him so hard I'm not sure how it's not hurting him, and a second later he comes with me.

His arms are unable to hold him up anymore so he settles his weight on top of me. "Am I too heavy?" he asks breathlessly.

"No, never." I snuggle deeper with him and close my eyes.

You will never be too much.

6

JEAN

Waking up the next morning should be blissful, amazing, but we awaken to the sound of an alarm going off in the house.

Before I can roll over, Jackson is out of bed and pulling on his sweatpants, a gun firmly in his hands.

"What's going on?" I ask, slipping out of bed too and putting on clothes in a hurry. Jackson walks to a screen on the wall, looking at the surveillance cameras.

"It's your dad and two women." He sighs and disables the alarm.

"Oh." I wince because I'm not sure if he's ready to meet the madness that is my family. "Well, I guess it's as good a time as any?" I laugh it off.

He walks to the closet and throws on a shirt. "I just unlocked the gate. They'll be here any minute."

"Come here and give me some smooches before my dad decides to cock block us all day." I grumble at the fact. I just got a small piece of him and I want more.

Jackson gives me a look. "I am a grown-ass man. Your dad isn't cock blocking shit." His hand slowly drags down my back before fully gripping my ass, squeezing.

"Good luck with that, baby," I tease, kissing him one last time before I make my way downstairs, excited to see my parents and sister.

When my dad sees me coming down the stairs, his face lightens with a certain happiness that is only reserved for us girls.

I swing the door open. "What a surprise." I run straight into my dad's arms, hugging him, then my mom and sister.

"Well shit, sister, did you get a sugar daddy or what?" My sister Jennifer slides right past me into the house, and my mother nods as she takes in the house too.

"Chill, women, try not to act like hoodlums," my dad scolds the both of them, and I step past, letting them inside.

I shut the door, hugging Mom. "How did you know where I was?" I ask. I'm not sure how they knew where Jackson lives.

Mom looks at Dad, who shrugs his shoulders. I hear footsteps on the stairs, and as one we look up to see Jackson walking down the stairs, now dressed in jeans and a shirt.

My sister grips my arm. "You lucky bitch!" she hisses, giving me a look that would kill a lesser person, but I know deep down she's happy for me.

I look Jackson dead in the eye. "I know, right?"

His lips curl up slightly, and he walks straight to my dad, shaking his hand. I can see both of their arms flexing as they squeeze the shit out of each other.

Men are such weird creatures.

"Are y'all done trying to break each other's hands or not? I want to meet the guy who kidnapped my daughter," my mom—Janna—tells the both of them.

Jackson looks amused and lets my dad's hand go, stepping back to face my mother. "It's very nice to meet you. I see where Jean got her looks from." He takes her hand gently.

Oh, he is good.

She blushes, giggling slightly. "I definitely can see how now."

My dad steps beside her, pulling her into his side and glaring at Jackson. Every guy that has met my father in the past has been deathly afraid. Usually I didn't see them again once they have their official meet.

I don't know what he tells them, but he takes them outside for the talk and then, bam, that's the end of it.

"This is my sister Jennifer. This is Jackson, my…" I trail off, wanting him to fill in.

"Your man, darlin'," he finishes, giving me that million-dollar smile, his dimples popping out. He is a total lady killer.

One by one all of us women sigh in sync. His beauty is something texts and pictures don't do justice.

"It's nice to meet you. Remember, if you hurt her, I will be your worst nightmare," my sister warns him.

Jackson takes it all in stride.

"Want me to make you guys some breakfast?" he offers, walking into the kitchen. The house has an open floor plan, which I love.

He is sweet. I love that he's trying.

I look at my mother. She has a soft look on her face and I know she's thinking along the same lines as me.

"Actually, Jackson, I need to speak to you about some things." My dad's voice changes when he says this.

"I can make breakfast if you guys want to go talk." I try to play it off like it doesn't bother me.

But it does.

I know deep down that this has something to do with me and Gary. Why else would my dad make the trip down here like this?

I watch them retreat to the back of the house where Jackson's office is located.

Jackson

I sit at my desk. Fredrick, Jean's dad, sits in front of me. He pulls out a manila envelope and slides it towards me.

"This was sent to me last night through my email."

I open it and I pull out the contents. Pictures scatter across my desk. Fuck.

They are pictures of what happened between me and Jean last night. There is a shit ton of pictures of me eating her out.

This shit was sent to her dad.

This is fucked up beyond measure.

I look at him, covering the pictures so that shit isn't right in his face.

"He also left me a note." He nods to a single piece of paper.

The note reads, "Do you see what a whore your daughter has turned into?" The paper crumples in my fist.

I thought I was angry last night?

This is a whole different level. No one disrespects and degrades her like this. "Is this her ex?" I almost don't recognize my own voice

"You know it fucking is." He rubs his face hard, trying to avoid the pictures at all costs.

I feel bad for him. I can't fucking fathom getting pictures like this of my daughter sent to me.

That is horribly fucking wrong and I am going to kill him. There is no doubt about that.

The shit he's playing is going to end.

"I don't want to tell her about this. She doesn't need that kind of pain, and knowing that you saw her like that would kill her," I tell Fredrick.

I want to protect her. I want her to forget that fucker even existed, like he just dropped off the face of the earth.

Which is going to happen.

"I agree with you. Jean is a tough girl and I'm proud of her for that, but she's soft inside just like her momma." He sits back in his seat, grinning, "I met her mother when I had her arrested for beating up some chick. I forgot what it was even about, honestly. I never took her to jail. I took her to my house and she never left."

He looks me dead in the eyes. "My baby likes you, I can see that. Take care of her. If I lost her or she got hurt, I don't think I could survive. Those girls are my whole entire world."

He scoots closer. "Me trusting you with that, my whole life, just know what you have in your hands."

At that, he leaves me reeling. I respect him. I respect how he has taken care of Jean her whole life, but now it's my turn. I will take care of her until I die.

7

JEAN

ONE MONTH LATER

Life here in Raleigh, Texas has been everything I had hoped for and more. Right now we're babysitting Chrystal and Kyle's daughter Cassandra.

Jackson is lying on the couch with her tucked into his side, her small head resting on his chest.

Can I say I have baby fever?

I think that's certain. My ovaries are clenching right now wanting him to impregnate me.

Could it be too soon?

Probably.

But I don't think I will be anywhere else than right here with him for the rest of my life. I can see myself marrying him, having a bunch of babies and having that white picket fence shit.

He would make the best dad to a bunch of little boys that will look exactly like him. His calm demeanor but fiery temper.

Let's not get into what it would be like to have another one of me, because I'm not sure the world can withstand it.

"She is so beautiful." I sit down beside him, running my hand down her sleeping back.

Jackson looks down at her, his face showing how much he loves her. I love that every guy in the club somehow has a hand in raising her.

Instead of it taking a village to raise a child, it's more like a whole biker club with big badass softies.

Is it wrong of me to want to bring my babies up in this life? I have grown to love every single member of this club.

"She is." He kisses the top of her fuzzy little head, my heart crying at such a beautiful view.

"Kind of gives you baby fever, doesn't it?" I laugh like what I'm saying could potentially open a lot of doors.

He gives me a look. "Is that a hint, baby?"

I play innocent. "Uh, no," I say dramatically.

He arches a disbelieving eyebrow. "Cassandra is so precious, it can't be helped." He stands up and gently places Cassandra in her Pack N Play.

"I got you something, doll."

I follow Jackson upstairs to our room. He takes a box out of the closet and hands it to me. "You didn't have to get me anything."

He crosses his arms across his chest. "Open it, sweetheart."

I do as he asks, dying to see what he got me. I pull off the lid and I come face to face with something that is as sacred as marriage.

A cut with the words "Property Of Jackson" on the back of it. My eyes sting and I try to hold back the tears that are threatening to spill.

This is huge in the biker world. There is no higher privilege than this. There's no mistaking when I wear this that I belong to him.

"I take it back."

He looks shocked. I grip the cut out of the box and pull it to my chest. "You did have to get me this. Took your ass long enough."

"Get your ass up here and kiss your man, your ole man."

Oh, how I love the sound of that.

I kiss him, just barely teasing him. "You will be getting your present later." I cup him through his jeans, feeling him harden beneath my fingers.

The doorbell rings. "I promised Chrystal I'd go shopping with her."

"Baby, you know that you need someone to be with you."

I put my hand up. "Yes, we have two prospects going with us," I reassure him. He's gotten more protective over me the last month.

He takes my cut from me and holds it open for me to slip my arms into. "You have never looked more beautiful, my girl." He kisses my forehead, once, twice, before he allows me to walk downstairs.

I open the front door and let in Kyle, who is going to spend the day with Jackson. "Ready, girl?" Chrystal asks.

"See you later, Kyle. We just put her down, so she should be out for a while," I tell him as I walk out the door, swinging my purse over my shoulder.

"I love the cut." Chrystal winks.

"Oh, how I love yours."

We both laugh and get in the back of an SUV. Both prospects are sitting in the front. They're newer and I haven't gotten to know them yet, but I take the prospects with a grain of salt. They rarely make it past the first month or so.

Chrystal and I walk in front of the prospects. I love how everyone stops and stares at us, avoiding eye contact.

This is the power of the Devils Souls, their presence affects everyone around them one way or another.

We dip into the first store as both of us need new jeans and we spend the next hour combing through everything.

The prospects stand at the entrance, which is fucking foolish. The guys are going to be pissed, because they always seem to have a way of knowing everything.

"I'm going to try these on," I tell Chrystal, who nods. I slip into the dressing room, which is basically just a curtain covering a closet.

I see feet standing in front of my curtain, which is closed, but I know it's a man out there. I guess the stupid prospect is finally doing this job.

I turn around to face the mirror and start to take off my pants when the curtain is ripped open and I come face to face with Gary.

What the fuck?

He has a gun in his hand. I look at the Glock and see that he has the safety on while he points it at me.

"We are fucking leaving, bitch," he hisses, grabbing ahold of my arm and pulling me out of the dressing room.

I could have stopped him, made a scene, but no, I'm not going to be a damsel. I'm going to allow him to take me.

I saw the report my dad sent to Jack. I'm not the first woman he has done this to and some of them have gone missing.

So I play along.

"Please don't do this, Gary!" I plead, putting my hands up to cover my mouth like I'm trying not to cry.

He drops his gun slightly, taking my cries seriously. He drags me towards the back of the building where there's an emergency exit.

Now if the prospects were doing their job, this wouldn't have happened. But I want to end this, so if I have to play victim for that to happen?

So be it.

I allow him to take me to the car, putting up enough fight so it doesn't look like I'm going freely. He doesn't know that I have a little bitty pistol in my boot and a small knife under my boob.

He throws me into the back seat way too hard for someone

who is barely fighting. That's another strike on his very long list.

Jackson is going to be so pissed when he finds out what happened to me. I do feel kind of shitty that I'm doing this willingly in a way.

I just want it over, and Jean is no damsel.

Jackson

My phone rings at the clubhouse and I take it out, expecting it to be Jean calling me, but it's Chrystal. I know in a split second that something is wrong.

"What happened?" I demand, already heading to the front door.

Chrystal is sobbing and I put it on speaker. "I can't find her! She went to the dressing room but she's not there." She is hysterical.

Kyle has a look of pain on his face, but I can't breathe, my chest hurts. I'm so numb. I take off to my bike, driving to the place that she was at. Maybe it was a mistake?

I can barely drive. My hands are shaking so bad I can barely grip the handle bars. Please, god, let it be a mistake.

If it's not? Hell hath no fury like a devil whose woman has been taken.

Jean

I pretend-sob all the way to wherever Gary's taking me, which isn't far. We've barely been in the car for five minutes when he stops outside of an abandoned house.

I lean back in the seat, trying to kick out at him with little effort as he rips open the door and tries to grab me.

If he truly believes me then he is more stupid than I was led to believe, because I kicked his ass already once with just a dildo.

I stumble along as he pulls me inside. He throws me down into a seat and ties me, barely. I can twist my wrist around in the knots.

Did I mention that my daddy taught me how to get out of every single kind of kidnapping situation?

Gary is so stupid I almost feel sorry for him and this pitiful excuse of a job he's doing. He runs to the front of the abandoned building, slamming the door shut.

He slowly turns to look at me, trying to be dramatic and intimidate me. It's almost laughable.

I let the fake tears run down my face. "Finally I've gotten you back, honey, are you okay? Did he force you to do anything?" he rushes out so fast that it makes my head spin.

Okay, he is worse off than I ever imagined. Does he really think that I wasn't with Jackson intentionally?

Gary stumbles closer and I try not to throw up in his face. It truly makes me sick that I was actually with him.

I shudder at the fact. I really had some whiskey goggles on or something.

"Oh thank you for rescuing me!" I gush out, acting like I'm so relieved.

Gary smiles happily. "I knew you missed me." He steps closers and I try to look innocent and happy.

I don't have an innocent bone in my body.

"Oh yes I did, Gary boy," I cry, shaking my head side to side like I'm crying but I'm really laughing.

This is *hilarious*.

Are you telling me that people have stressed over this stupid motherfucker? Because I feel kind of stupid right now.

"There there." He makes a shushing sound, trying to soothe me and stop me from crying. Bitch, these are tears of freaking joy.

"I can forgive what I witnessed, what he did to you on that bike of his." I can hear the disgust in his voice.

Well shit, he witnessed that?

At least he finally saw what it looks like when a woman orgasms. "I'm sure you had no choice. Now let me get this off of you." He takes out a knife and moves to cut my binds.

My head snaps up, a grin on my face. His expression changes to one of shock. "I don't think so, fucker." I kick out at him, hitting him in the knee, and I stand up, the rope falling to the ground.

I bend over and grab my gun from my boot. "Get your ass in the chair." My hand is steady as I aim it at him. I have my safety on.

He does as he is told, his eyes full of fury. I spot duct tape on the counter, which is going to do just fine.

"If you move, I will blow your brains out."

He nods and just allows me to put duct tape on him. I use the whole roll. He's not going anywhere anytime soon.

I take out my phone that he never even bothered to take from me, and his eyes widen once he sees it.

"You're so stupid. I faked the whole thing so I can get rid of you once and for all."

I watch as a hundred different emotions show on his face. He realizes that he's caught and that these are probably his last moments on earth.

I don't think I would have it in me to kill him, but I'm going to make him wish that he was. I know Jackson can follow through.

I dial Jackson, who answers almost instantly. "Jean?!" he says frantically. My heart fractures at the sound of him so scared.

"I'm okay, baby. He's taken me to the abandoned house right outside of town behind the T mart. He's the stupidest kidnapper ever. I have him tied up with duct tape," I rush out so I can settle his nerves.

He does the unthinkable: he laughs. "Fuck, baby, I am so mad at you. We'll be there in a few minutes." He doesn't hang up the phone. I put it on speakerphone and set it down on the counter.

Jackson addresses Gary. "So you're going to answer all of my questions. If not you're going to wish that you listened to me."

He doesn't respond but just watches me. "What happened to the girls that are missing?"

At that Gary grins. "They didn't listen to me. I had to correct the problem," he says so easily, like he's talking about checking the mail.

I take my knife out and spot his hand and I sit down on the ground. I grin as I start to make small little cuts on his hands, until every single patch of skin is covered.

Then I walk into the kitchen, humming, finding different things that will cause pain. Rubbing salt into the wound? That seems fitting right now.

I sit back down. "You know it's ironic, you'll be the next missing person but no one will ever find you. I will make sure you are in pieces. You will be pig shit. Like the piece of shit you are."

I pour the salt over his hand, rubbing harder and harder, making sure to grind it deeply into his cuts.

He starts to scream and tries to back away from me. I laugh because he sounds like a pig. "You sound exactly what you're going to be lunch for," I taunt him.

"I think you'll look better with ear piercing, don't you think?" I spot a nail on the floor. I'm sure it's really dull, but with enough force that shit won't matter.

I walk up behind him and slowly push the nail through his ear. "You tortured me for a month, this is nothing!" I yell.

"I am going to kill you, rape you and do so many bad things to you!" he spits out, and he stops halfway through his rant, his eyes wide, when Jackson fills the room along with his brothers in the MC.

What I mean by filling the room is his anger fills every single crevice. "Oh please continue, tell me what you had planned for *my* woman." Jackson says, slowly walking towards him, then grips Gary's throat. "Tell me!" he roars in his face.

"I was going to use her over and over until her body just gives out. She is mine and she will always be mine." Gary taunts him, and my stomach filled with disgust.

Jackson smiles sadistically. "Good answer." Then he turns to look at me. "Look away, sweet girl."

I turn away, then bam, then the sound of nothing. I turn around to see brain splatting the floor behind Gary, a single hole in the center of his forehead.

Jackson reaches out and takes me, pulling me to him. "Did you really put fucking salt in his wound?" He looks to the ground at the salt spilled there.

"Kind of ironic, isn't it? Too bad he didn't have a dildo, huh?" I wink at Jackson.

Everyone in the room laughs. The story is a legend with the guys.

We all leave, leaving him there for the rats, bugs and the other creatures.

We never speak of what happened again, leaving the past in the past.

Another person's crazy is another person's normal.

Ours is a little of both.

EPILOGUE

EIGHTEEN YEARS LATER

"Trixie, where is your brother?" I ask her once I get home from grocery shopping. She's doing her homework on the dining room table.

She looks at me, both eyebrows arched. "How am I supposed to know? Keeping up with him is definitely not something I like to do." She curls her mouth in disgust.

Dear Jesus, give me the strength. She is eleven years old but she has the attitude of someone who is much older.

Karma is a bitch.

I give her my mom glare until she relents. "Last time I saw him he was walking towards the guest house."

"Thank you, baby." I kiss the top of her head.

I walk out to the guest house that Matthew has pretty much moved into because he thinks he is a grown man and needs his space.

I grab the door handle and throw it open. "Matthew, I need you to help me carry this table." I stop dead in my tracks as the image in front of me is branded deep into my mind, never leaving me.

My child, my baby boy, on the ground, his face buried between Morgan's legs—Morgan is the daughter of our friends—and Trenton Torch's son's face deep in her tits.

I don't speak.

I turn around, shut the door, and walk back into the house, forgetting the table.

What the fuck is happening?

My child walks into the house like I just didn't witness what I just witnessed. "What did you mean, Mom?" He grins, looking so much like his father it's sickening.

"Lock the door next time, yeah?" I grumble.

"Sorry, Mom," he says, laughing slightly, totally unfazed. "I love youuu," he says in a sweet tone, acting much younger than his seventeen years.

"If you come over here and touch me, I will stab you with this fork!" I scream when he gets too close to me.

He falls to the ground laughing.

How will I ever survive?

Jackson walks into the house and takes in the scene. He looks to Trixie but she's just as confused as to what's happening.

"What the fuck?"

Matthew laughs harder. "Mom walked in on us," he manages to get out through his fits. I will never be the same again.

Jackson laughs and walks over, wrapping his arms around me. "My baby isn't a baby anymore," I cry as that fact hits me. Then Matthew starts over again and I pick up the fork.

He holds his hands up, smiling.

I close my eyes and groan into Jackson's chest.

"You're lucky I love you, Matty."

He smiles happily, his dad's smile. "I love you too, Mom. Thank you for accepting the fact...you know," he says simply.

I jolt at what he's saying. "Of course, baby, I'd support you no matter what in life." Not crossed out anymore, I hug him.

"Touch me with your hands and you will die!" I scream when he tries to wrap his arms around me.

That sets them off laughing again.

God help me.

RYAN

PROLOGUE

MYRA

I'M SO glad to be finally off of work. This day has been long. I had two women go into labor today at almost exactly the same time, which is rare.

That also means that my babysitter had to stay longer than she planned—it's almost time for my baby Mia to go to bed.

Mia is eighteen months old and she is the best thing that ever happened to me. She's my everything.

My ex-boyfriend got caught up with drugs and he didn't want anything to do with her, so I made him sign his rights over. It was as simple as that.

She's all mine. I'm a single mother and it's hard, but I would not change a thing.

I feel like a shitty mother because I have to work so much— the mom guilt is real. It doesn't help that women mom-shame all of the time, but I have to take care of her. That's the most important thing and I am beyond thankful that I can provide that for her.

I walk up the walkway to my house and I put the key in the lock, but much to my surprise, it just opens.

Okay, I'm going to have to talk to the babysitter about that.

She's supposed to have the door locked and the alarm set when she's here.

I don't live in a bad part of town by any means, but I'd rather be safe than sorry.

I step inside the house and I find it completely silent, which is weird. Having a boisterous eighteen-month-old usually means a noisy home.

I turn the corner and every single part of my body freezes at the sight before me. There's a man standing above my babysitter Debbie, pointing a gun straight at her face, and my beautiful baby is sitting beside her, her eyes wide.

Oh my god.

Without hesitation, I take out my gun. I always carry one with me. My purse scrapes against the wall, making a sound that could be an explosion in this so-very-silent house.

The man's eyes widen and I notice the cut on his jacket. He's the son of the Satans Rejects President.

His gun moves from Debbie straight to my daughter. "No!" I yell, getting his attention, and I raise my gun, just as he points his at me.

Got you.

I pull the trigger, hitting him in the middle of his stomach before he can take a shot at me. He falls to the floor and I run over, taking his gun away from him before he can do anything else.

I'm not sure I'm even breathing. My heart hurts and I'm so terrified, I barely manage to take out my phone and dial 911. I scoop up my daughter, who clings to me, her little body shaking.

This is all too much. He had a gun on my baby! The thought of something ever happening to her…it steals the air from my lungs.

I carry her out of the house into the front yard in case he isn't dead and gathers some superhuman strength to get up.

I don't even bother checking on the babysitter. I don't give a fuck about her at this point because I have a feeling in my gut that this happened because of her.

She stumbles out onto the porch, falling to her knees and trying to catch her breath. I get inside of my car in case I need to make a run for it, waiting for the police and ambulance to show up.

Hours, minutes later, I don't even know how long it is, but they finally show up. I get out of my car and explain what's going on, and they run inside of the house to check on the man lying there.

The babysitter backs up my story but she adds in her own—she owed the man money and he came to take it one way or another.

I eye the bitch. I'm pissed. I trusted her to take care of my baby—the most precious thing in my life.

Hours later the police leave, leaving me alone in my house. I don't want to stay here anymore considering what happened. I'll start looking for a new place tomorrow. The quicker I'm out of here, the better.

Mia climbs into my bed and I don't resist. I want my baby close with me tonight. I close my eyes and command myself to fall asleep. I'll worry about everything tomorrow.

~

I drop Mia off at my mother's house for a few hours. Today my rage isn't any better. Actually I think it's worse because I've had time to think on it.

I have one purpose in mind today and that is to track down Debbie, my babysitter.

I pull up in front of her house. I've never been here before and I see it's run-down, way more than I expected it to be for someone who gets paid very well to watch my girl.

I walk up to her front porch, pounding my fist on the door. I can hear her running to open it.

Debbie looks out the small window next to her door before unlocking it and I push her inside of her house.

"What are you doing here?" she asks, taking a few steps away from me, looking confused.

I slip my purse off of my shoulder onto the floor, and her eyes follow my movements as I throw my hair into a bun next.

"I'm here to beat your ass," I deadpan.

Her eyes widen in disbelief. She turns around, trying to run out of the room, but I catch her by her hair, pulling her back to me.

She tries to pry my hands from her hair, falling down to her knees. "Please, don't do this," she begs, tears in her eyes.

I want to feel sorry for her, but I can't muster that emotion. My baby is my everything and she put her in danger.

"Tell me why this happened then! You could have killed my baby!" I yell in her face, tightening my grip in her hair.

"I borrowed money from them when I shouldn't have. I didn't think not paying them back would result in that. I thought they were just empty threats," Debbie whispers, trying to make herself as small as possible.

"Still doesn't change the fact I'm going to beat your ass," I laugh, and pull her head back with a snap of her hair, I bring my fist down once, twice, three times before I let her fall to the ground, disgusted by her.

"Now I feel better. If I see you again, I won't stop next time." I glare at her and she nods her head in understanding.

I pick up my purse off the ground, slamming the door behind me as I walk out to my car.

A guy on a motorcycle drives past, and I stop in my tracks when I spot the patch on the back. Satan's Rejects.

Oh shit.

I get in my car, locking the door behind me. Goose bumps

break out across my skin. That's not a good thing, I think to myself, especially after what happened.

I pull out and look in my rearview mirror, and I see the bike pulling up in Debbie's yard.

Not my problem. No way in hell am I going back to help her.

1

MYRA

ONE MONTH LATER

It's official, I'm scared. It started off small—I would see Satan's Rejects in random places in town and I just thought that I had very shitty luck.

Then when I left work, they would be parked close by just watching me. That freaked me the fuck out. My mother has been watching Mia for me as I work, but I've been scared to leave her.

But now? It's really hit home. I found a letter on my bed. I've gotten voice mails, weird ones that I can't explain, but it's happened so many times that it can't be a coincidence.

Beautiful daughter you have.

I would hate to have anything happen to her.

I felt fear, fear so deep that I could taste it. It was so deep rooted I thought my heart was going to stop in my chest. They didn't threaten me.

They threatened my baby.

I have to run. I know the only place that may help me, but I know it would come at a cost. I heard about a MC that protects women. It's a couple of towns over and it's my only hope.

I don't think the police could handle this. Plus, I want these motherfuckers to feel pain, and sitting in jail isn't going to solve anything.

I want Mia to have the best protection, and if I've got to take that out in my blood, I will do that.

I hurry and pack a suitcase. Mia's in the living room playing with some dolls. I pack enough to get us by for a couple of weeks and I'll buy more if needed.

"Baby, come pick out some toys. We're going on a trip!" I yell for her, and she runs into her room, gathering toys by the armful.

I have to tell my mother what happened and that I'm leaving, I just don't think it's safe to tell her where until I know Mia isn't in danger.

I don't want to go, but I feel like I need to get help or just run somewhere and start over.

It's a fucking MC. I shot a member of their fucking club. I'm sure that's not something that's easily forgivable.

I call my mother and she takes it really hard. It breaks my heart to have her in such pain, but what can I do?

I finish packing and putting everything in my SUV. I look at my house, feeling sad that I'm leaving here—this is where I raised my baby for eighteen months.

I walk back inside of the house and pick up Mia. "You ready for your road trip?" I ask her, kissing her cheek.

She grins, her little dimple popping out on her right cheek. "Yes, Mommy, let's go!" She throws her little fist in the air, giggling.

I carry her out of the house, locking the door behind me. I put her in her car seat and hand her a sippy cup of milk. She'll be out in minutes.

With one last look at my home, I pull out and make the two-hour trip to the MC. This could go well or it could be a total disaster. Maybe the rumors aren't true. Maybe they're just as bad as the Rejects.

But I have to have faith. I have to pray that they will protect my daughter.

~

NOT ONCE ON THE DRIVE THERE DO I SEE A BIKE. I MAKE SURE I'M not followed. Mia has slept almost the whole drive and I pull up outside the gate at the MC.

A guy manning the gate walks over to me and I roll down my window. "I need to speak to your president," I manage to get out without my voice shaking.

He looks at me, confused, then talks into a radio. He opens the gate after a voice replies.

He points to the front of the building and tells me where to park. I make my way there, trying to talk myself out of turning around.

The guy opens the car door for me. "Thank you." I look down at his vest and see "Jack" on the front. "Jack," I finish.

He smiles and I open the back door, grabbing my bag with the evidence, along with my degree. Mia smiles at me happily, lifting her arms for me to take her.

I close my eyes and hold her tight, breathing her scent. *You got this, Myra.* I let Jack lead me inside the club.

The first thing I notice is that it's huge, it's open and has a bar, a sitting area, eating area and a game area. The outside doesn't give a hint to what it looks like inside. Inside it's almost like a house.

Jack leads me down a hallway, farther away from the exit and my car. Mia is still tired from the trip and is lying on my shoulder, completely unfazed.

He stops outside a door and knocks. "Come in!" I hear someone yell.

Jack pushes the door open and I see a man sitting behind a

desk. He's wearing a cut with the word "President" on a patch in the front, along with the name Kyle.

Kyle looks at me and then at my daughter. "Come on in." He smiles, and it makes him look a little less scary, but I won't be fooled. These men are dangerous and that's all there is to it.

I sit down in the chair in front of his desk. I shift Mia until she's resting against my chest. She grabs the blanket, tucking it under her neck.

"What can I do for you?" he asks as Jack leaves us alone.

I gather my courage. "I need protection. It's not just me being threatened but my little girl. I had a babysitter who owed Satan's Rejects money. They followed her to my house and I walked in on a guy who had his gun trained on my daughter along with the sitter." I stop, sucking in a deep breath. "I shot him to protect my daughter. The police came. He lived, but he was the son of the President." Kyle's eyes widen as he listens.

I open my bag and hand him the letter they left me along with my phone so he can listen to the voicemails. Kyle reads the letter and listens to the voicemails, then looks at me and my daughter. "I'm a doctor. I could offer assistance if needed for the protection." I throw it out there. I'm not sure if that's going to help my case, but isn't that how it works? They do back shit and they want to keep it under the radar.

Kyle sets the paper down and I hand him my doctorate degree next. He studies it and hands it back to me. "I can't give you a yes or no answer; this is for the guys to vote in the club."

I nod, because this is fair and it's a lot of people to take on, especially for someone they don't even know.

"Just hang out here while I call the guys in."

∼

An hour later Kyle comes and gets me, letting me know

that they're ready for me. I follow behind him and walk into a room filled with a shit ton of huge, bulking men.

Mia sits up and looks around the room for a second before wiggling, wanting down. I set her down. She walks straight to the guy closest to me. I look at the name on his vest. Ryan.

Ryan is beautiful, one of the hottest men I have ever seen, with his dark brown hair, green eyes and tan skin. He's huge—one of the biggest men in the room.

Mia walks over to him, her arms raised. He smiles at her and picks her up. She lays her head on his shoulder, completely content.

Oh my. I start over to take her. "I can take her," I tell him, and Ryan finally looks at me and jumps in his seat like I shocked him.

Huh, that's weird.

Ryan continues to stare at me like I'm his long-lost best friend. "You can sit here," a guy on the other side of Ryan says.

I thank him and take the seat next to Ryan so I can be close to my baby. I look at Kyle, who is staring at the three of us, amused.

"Myra, explain everything," Kyle tells me.

So I do that. I start from the beginning and tell everyone and why I'm here. I look at my daughter, innocent in all of this. It would kill me if something happened to her.

I'm exhausted; I haven't slept for more than an hour or two in god knows how long. I was so scared that they would break in in the middle of the night. I'm an independent woman, but I also know my limits.

Kyle looks at every guy in the room, and one by one they nod. "We will provide protection in exchange for your services."

My eyes widen in disbelief. I'd hoped that this would happen, but actually hearing it, it's like I can finally breathe after being underwater.

Ryan looks at me fully. "Where's your man?" he asks in his gruff voice.

I shake my head. "He's on drugs, not that I knew that at the time. He signed his rights over. He's out of the picture." I smile at him, Ryan jumps again like I shocked him.

Is he okay?

"I need to put you in one of the safe houses instead of the center because you have a job." Kyle rubs his chin, thinking.

"No, she stays with me," Ryan tells everyone.

I gape at him in disbelief. "What?"

He rubs my daughter's back gently. My eyes follow his movements because it's hard to believe a man who looks like him, as tough as he is, can be tender. "My house has top-notch security. Plus, I can protect you and Mia."

Okay, that got me. I will take everything I can get for my daughter, I don't care what it takes. Being scared for me is one thing, but fear for your child is stifling.

"If you're sure..." I trail off.

Mia finally raises her head. "Bite bite," she announces. It's time for dinner.

"Do you need anything else?" Ryan asks Kyle.

"We've covered everything."

Ryan stands up with Mia and she's tugging on his dog tags, studying them. He looks at me. "Let's go get her fed."

I blink, once, twice. I just can't wrap my head around all of this, but more so him. I grab my bags and follow him out the door.

My daughter is fully content having him walk her through the clubhouse. She doesn't see him as a stranger and I'm happy that she's a confident little lady, but it scares me because she's too trusting.

We step outside and Ryan opens my SUV door, placing Mia in her seat. "Let's grab something at the diner, then we need to go shopping and get kid shit."

I laugh because his gruff language is pretty hilarious. He looks at me, a small smile on his lips. "Follow me, yeah?" His voice is much softer this time, he moves away from us and slides on his bike, looking back at us one last time.

He peels out of the lot, his arms flexing as he speeds off onto the highway. I know one thing: it's going to be hard living with that beast of a man.

But I have been known to be a glutton for punishment—look at my fucking ex. I knew he was shit, but what did I do anyway? Made a baby. But I feel like Ryan is different than anything I have ever known.

Gone are the pretty boys. Hello bad boys on a bike. I like looking at the latter a hell of a lot more.

2

MYRA

MIA IS SINGING along with the radio in the back seat, making the words up along the way. She's adorable.

I feel so much better. I have so much relief in my heart that I got the protection that I needed.

The guys were different than I expected. Don't get me wrong, I was so scared walking into that room with all of those men, but the moment my daughter ran straight to Ryan, who picked her up without a thought, my attitude changed.

I watch as he pulls into a cute little diner that has a sixties vibe to it. Through the window I see a waitress on roller skates.

How cute is this?

I pull up beside Ryan and he climbs off his bike. My eyes immediately go to his ass. His jeans are tight, showing his butt.

My god.

Ryan opens my door for me, his eyes going all around us to make sure it's safe. He takes my hand and helps me out.

"Why thank you," I flirt, smiling at him fully because it was cute that he opened my door for me.

He rolls his eyes and then moves to the back, pulling out Mia and holding her in his arms. Her hand goes straight to his dog tags.

He looks down at her, smiling. Wow, what a beautiful smile he has. It lights up his whole face.

I try not to smile at the sight of the two of them together, which I know is probably wild at this point because I just met him, but I'm not blind. Seeing this gorgeous man holding my daughter puts me and every woman around at risk of ovary explosion.

He holds the door open for the both of us and leads us towards the back of the diner away from everyone else. He slides Mia into the booth and he climbs in beside her.

Okay, I didn't expect that.

I sit in front of them, and Ryan without a second thought hands her a kids menu for her to color on.

"Do you have any kids? Wife?" How stupid of me to not even ask, because I would feel shitty for checking him out if he was taken.

"Neither."

Well, okay then. I open my menu and my eyes go straight to the burgers, I haven't had one of those in god knows how long.

To break the silence, I put down my menu, looking at Ryan. "I think I'm going to put in for a job…maybe just part-time?" I tell him.

But then I forget—who's going to watch my daughter? "Well, never mind. I forgot I don't have a sitter anymore. Hmm." I brush my hair over my shoulder, deep in thought.

"I can watch her, or you can use the sitter that watches Cassandra. She's Kyle's daughter."

"That's a good idea." I smile at him. His eyes go to my mouth and his eyes soften.

I'm getting to him.

"Ry-Ry." Mia tugs on Ryan's white T-shirt to get his attention. He turns to her and she points to a scribble on the coloring page. She mumbles in baby talk. "That's pretty," he tells her.

She beams at him happily. My poor heart. She hands him a blue crayon, wanting him to color with her.

He takes it without hesitation, coloring with her. My daughter hasn't really had any male interaction because her father isn't in her life. I'm sure I could have tried more, but I know she'd suffer more if he was in and out of her life all of that time, demanding money.

He was a lawyer when we first got together and then he just couldn't cover it anymore. He lost his job and then the drugs just took over everything…his temper took over.

The last straw was when I wouldn't enable him anymore. I was eight months pregnant. He wanted more money to get more drugs, but I just couldn't give it to him. I feared for my safety and my unborn child.

So I cut him off just like his family had done.

He flipped his shit, throwing things around my house, breaking everything.

I called the police on him and he was taken to jail.

Then when Mia was born, I had him sign all of his rights away. She needs someone who can be a father figure for her, Not a someday, once-in-a-while kind of dad.

But she is involved with his family. I allow her to stay all night with them once every couple of months when her dad is gone away for a while. During the summer she gets to stay a week. We make it work.

"What can I get you guys?" The waitress breaks me from my depressing thoughts. We order our food and I watch Mia, She is coloring on the paper without a care in the world and I envy her for that.

"You did the right thing," Ryan says out of the blue.

I tilt my head to the side slightly, confused. "What do you mean?" I ask.

"You protected her and yourself, you did the right thing. You're a good-ass mom because you're still doing what it takes to keep her safe."

Damn, that felt unbelievable. I didn't realize how much I needed for someone to tell me that. Stress has eaten me alive since all of this happened. Nothing feels worse than thinking you're failing as a mother.

"Thank you, Ryan, that means a lot," I tell him honestly, and he nods, turning his attention back to my daughter, who is having him color with her.

Our food comes and I reach for Mia's plate to cut her burger up for her so it's easier for her to eat, but Ryan does it before I can even reach over.

I bite my lip. "There you go, sweetheart," he tells her and pushes her plate over. "Thank you, Ry-Ry."

I wonder about the center. I think I would like to volunteer my services to whoever needs it there. "Does the center take volunteers?" I ask Ryan.

He nods. "Wanting to volunteer?"

"Yeah, I think I would like to as long as I can bring Mia with me. "

"That won't be an issue. I can watch her if you ever need me too." He smiles and hands her a napkin when she gets ketchup on her finger. She takes it and wipes her finger but misses almost all of it.

He laughs and cleans her hand for her. "All done."

She giggles and sticks her finger in ketchup again. I smother my laughter. He pretends to glare at her; she glares right back at him.

He laughs and hands her another napkin, and she proceeds to do it herself this time.

I don't know how I feel about all of this. The second he met my daughter he was hands-on and she went straight to him.

I won't argue because he's the one who's going to keep her safe.

Ryan leads us right outside of town to a gated community. My first thought the farther we drive along the highway is that the houses are absolutely beautiful.

He stops in front of another gate and inputs a code. The gate swings open and he drives down the driveway, which reveals a large beautiful southern-type home with a wraparound porch.

He motions for me to pull inside of the garage and it shuts behind us. I get out and pull Mia out of her seat while Ryan grabs our bags.

"Your house is beautiful." The kitchen is stainless steel with beautiful white cabinets with stainless steel appliances.

"Here are your rooms." We follow him up the stairs and he pushes open a door to a room that has a little toddler bed, "I had this delivered by one of the prospects while we were eating." He sets one of the smaller bags down.

Mia wiggles to be let down and she runs straight to some toys that I didn't realize were there.

"You didn't have to do all of this. I can pay you back for all of it." I reach inside of my purse to write him a check.

He lifts his hand. "No, I wanted to do this. She's going to be living here in my home where it's a strange place. I wanted her to feel as comfortable as possible. It's the least I can do."

Wow, that is the most he has ever spoken. I know when to fight my battles and when to fold. I know he won't budge on this going by the staredown he's giving me right now.

I reach forward and take a hold of his much larger hand. "Thank you very much. You have gone above and beyond what I was expecting. I will forever be grateful."

His face softens and I love seeing that on him, but more so because it's aimed at me. I wonder what other expressions I can inspire in him...

Stop, Myra, don't go down that rabbit hole. You may not make it out unscathed. I am also a woman who hasn't had sex since before my daughter was born, but even then calling it "sex" was a long shot.

"Your room is right next door and mine is down the hall next to the stairs. I'll let you guys get settled." He hands me my bag, leaving me alone with Mia, who is busy trying to open her new toys.

I sit down on the floor, my back leaning against the wall, exhausted. The fear will always be with me until all of this is fully over.

But right now I think I can finally breathe a little bit. I was drowning for so long. I look at my precious baby, who is so innocent, and thinking of someone wanting to hurt her makes me want to kill.

"What's the matter, Momma?" Mia asks, startling me. She sits down on my lap holding her baby.

I smooth her hair down her back. "Nothing, sweet girl, just tired." She plays with her dolls and allows me to hold her. I needed this moment to fully catch up with everything.

A couple of hours later I have our clothes put away, toiletries out and it's time for a snack for her before I put her into her bed.

She walks down the stairs with me holding her hand. We turn the corner to the kitchen and we see Ryan standing over the stove in a pair of sweatpants and a white T-shirt.

Sweet baby Jesus, who knew sweatpants could be so hot? He turns and looks at us. "Ry-Ry!" Mia calls and runs across the room to him. He picks her up and puts her on his hip.

"Did you have a good evening playing?" he asks her and looks up at me, his eyes moving from the top of my head to the tips of my feet.

I see the fire in his eyes; he likes what he sees. I can't hide the smirk and his expression drops, knowing he's caught.

"Is that pagettttti?" Mia yells out looking over Ryan's

shoulder at the stove. He plops her down gently on the counter opposite the stove. She claps her little hands together.

"Yes, I had a feeling you liked it." He winks at her.

He puts some on a plate, using a fork to cut the spaghetti into smaller pieces, and I know right then he's making it for her.

He's precious. I know that's not the ideal word for a specimen like him, but that's my first thought.

I walk over and try to help. "I can handle it if you want to eat?" I offer.

"If you want, you can make your plate." He finishes cutting up Mia's spaghetti and gives her a spoon to scoop it up.

It makes me wonder how he knew that it's easier this way for kids. "Can I ask you how you know so much about kids?" I can't resist the urge to ask.

"My sister has two kids. I babysit all the time."

That makes sense. "How old are they?" I ask, and make my plate along with Ryan's.

"Jake is eight and Olivia is six. My sister is a single mother, so I try to help her out as much as possible to give her breaks."

I put the plates on the table and Ryan carries Mia along with her plate, setting her up in the chair along with something to sit on so she can reach the table.

"That's really kind of you! Your sister sounds like she's a strong lady." Ryan studies me like he's trying to figure me out.

"She is and so are you. You did it alone too," he points out.

That takes all of the air out of the room. I'm speechless. "Thank you, that means a lot."

He doesn't say anything else, leaving me to my thoughts and they're mostly filled with Ryan and trying to figure him out.

3

MYRA

ONE WEEK LATER

I can't sleep. It's been a week since we moved in with Ryan and I can't relax. My body is still in fight or flight mode. Every little creak seems to happen the second I drift off to sleep.

I have taken to sleeping on the floor next to Mia's bed because that seems to the only way I can sleep.

I'm so afraid of something happening to her or not being there to protect her, I'm driving myself crazy.

She is sound asleep and I'm lying here staring at the ceiling. That's when I hear a creak outside the door, and I tense for the hundredth time tonight.

The door is pushed open and I see Ryan hovering at the door. I wait for him to leave but he doesn't. He comes into the room and sits down beside me.

"What are you doing?" I whisper. I sit up, rubbing my eyes.

"Lay down." He takes my pillow, fluffing it up and laying it on his lap. "Lay down. I'll watch over the both of you."

That is the sweetest thing anyone has ever done for me. I reach forward, resting my hand on his cheek. I can't speak right now because I'm not sure I can keep from crying.

My heart is a little less heavy tonight and it's because of Ryan. I don't feel so alone.

I lay down, closing my eyes, his smell drifting over me. I feel him shift as he rests against Mia's bed, then he pulls my blanket up my arm.

His hand settles in my hair, softly stroking, and I smile as I finally drift into a deep, deep sleep.

∽

I WAKE UP THE NEXT MORNING STILL WRAPPED IN RYAN'S ARMS, but he's lying with me, holding me tightly against his chest almost protectively.

I can't resist the urge to snuggle a little closer and bask in the feeling of being held.

He shifts under me and I peek up to see him staring at the ceiling. He looks down, catching me spying on him. I laugh and roll over onto my back, stretching my arms above my head before sitting up to look at Ryan.

"You're beautiful," he says sweetly. I lean forward, kissing him on the cheek. He has been so sweet to me since we moved in, I have quite a bit of a crush on him.

His hand comes to the back of my neck, not letting me move far away. I lick my lips, and his eyes move from my eyes to my lips.

Oh my god, is he going to kiss me?

He splits the very short amount of distance between us, pressing his lips against mine softly.

Heaven. That's my first thought as his lips glide over mine. I sigh and scoot closer, allowing him to kiss me fully, deeply.

I drag my fingers up, burying them deeply into his hair, which feels like silk beneath my fingers.

We both hear Mia sigh in her sleep, breaking the moment.

We look at each other deeply as his thumb rubs gently over my bottom lip. "Perfect."

I wrap my arms around his neck, resting my head against his shoulder. He holds me tightly and I let him. I don't want him to let me go. I feel safe.

"Momma." I look up and see Mia sitting up in bed with her little stuffed animal. I scoot away from Ryan and pick her up out of bed, cuddling her in between us.

"Good morning, my angel." I kiss the top of her head. She closes her eyes and leans her head against Ryan.

He smiles at her—he's fallen for her. No one can resist loving my Mia; she is precious. "Still tired, angel?" he asks her, pushing her very messy hair out of her face.

She nods and turns over on her side. Ryan picks her up, cuddling her against his chest, rocking her side to side like she's a little baby.

The sight makes me happy. "Let's go downstairs and nap on the couch," I suggest, seriously loving the idea of cuddling the both of them.

Ryan stands up, and I guess that means yes. I reach and grab Mia's blanket along with the one Ryan and I were sharing.

Mia is already back asleep and doesn't stir on the way downstairs. Ryan sits down on the couch and Mia scoots farther up until her head is right under his chin, her little fists grabbing ahold of his shirt.

"Come on." Ryan lifts his other arm and motions for me to snuggle up on the other side. I lift out the recliner for him so he can lay back and I do the same for me in the middle seat.

I cover all of us with the blanket and snuggle into his side, his warmth instantly comforting me.

I fall asleep, fully content for the first time in a long time.

Today I'm at the center and I'm giving exams and administering birth control. I see the number of women and men who have escaped horrible situations and it makes me sad.

It's even worse when I see the grim faces of the kids who have seen their mother or father being abused or have been abused themselves.

I'm thankful that they're here so they have a chance at making a better life for themselves. That makes me happy.

I'm growing to seriously love Chrystal. She is the sweetest and she cares about everyone here deeply and wants them to better themselves.

"Next!" I call and wait for my next patient to walk in. A young girl around eighteen or nineteen walks in. I can see the fear all over her face as she sits down.

I smile, trying to reassure her. "Are you okay, honey?" I ask her. She looks at the door then back at me.

"One of the men here who claims to have left an abusive relationship snuck over to the women's dorms and attacked one of the women last night, but she's too scared to come forward and I don't know what to do," she whispers urgently, like she's afraid he's going to burst through the door any minute.

This is a serious problem. I know the guys have hired security so that they don't even mix at all and they're in totally different buildings.

"It's okay, sweetheart. I'll get this handled."

She lets out a deep breath, trying to calm herself, then we move on to the other reason she came in here.

The second she leaves, I text Ryan who is sitting in the front of the building along with Chrystal.

This is a serious problem. A lot of the women are in a very fragile state and they don't need this fear wrapped in all of the shit they already have going on.

I feel like I need to speak to the woman and make sure she's okay, in all ways, and then I'll put Ryan on their ass to make them regret ever hurting a woman.

Ryan all but runs into the room, his eyes searching me up and down to make sure I'm okay. I probably should have mentioned that in my text.

Chrystal comes in next with Kyle on her tail, who closes the door behind him.

"We have a serious issue,. One of the girls here told me that a man snuck out of the men's dorm and attacked one of the women last night."

Chrystal gasps in shock and grabs Kyle's hand, who is pissed along with Ryan, but this needs to be handled delicately.

"I need to speak to her first to get to the bottom of it. We don't want to do more damage." I try to defuse the situation, even though I really don't want to. I'm going on instinct right now and I'm mad as hell.

"We need to check the cameras," Ryan voices, and I fully agree with that.

That's what they do. We stand and wait until we find what we're looking for—one of the new members of the center across the road manages to sneak in. He had it timed perfectly.

I wanted to think that this didn't happen but it did, and now I'm standing outside of this woman's—Christa's—bedroom waiting to walk in there to talk to her.

Sometimes I hate my job. I really don't want to ask her questions and maybe cause her pain, but for the sake of the other ladies, we have to because it's a fuck-up on our part too.

I knock and wait for her to open the door. She finally does and when she looks at me, I can see a small cut on her lip.

"Can I come in?" I ask, and she nods, letting me step inside, shutting the door behind us.

Christa sits on the bed and I sit down in the chair at the small desk that's in every room. "You found out, didn't you?" she asks in a small voice, her eyes focusing on her hands.

"We did, honey. Are you okay?" I resist the urge to take her hand because that may not be wanted.

"I am. He was my ex-boyfriend. I guess he just found a way in."

I close my eyes because this may be even worse than I feared. "I am so sorry, honey. We are going to take care of this problem. You're safe, okay? This won't ever happen again."

She nods and winces as she shifts on the bed, "Where does it hurt?" I ask and stand up.

"Just my side. He didn't get to do anything to me because that one girl interrupted. He just hit me a bit."

I'm relieved that it's not as bad as I feared, but I'm still sad nonetheless. I can't help but imagine what would happen if someone was mean to my baby girl someday. I would truly kill someone, without a doubt.

Christa lifts up her shirt and I see the bruising right on her side and fingerprint marks on her arm.

Just as I finish examining her, the door bangs open, scaring me and her both. A man is standing there and I recognize him from the video footage of last night. This is the man who harmed her.

Oh shit.

I step in front of her. "Go into the bathroom," I tell her. There is no way I'll allow him to harm her again.

She hesitates but does as I ask. I hear the door click and then the twist of the lock, leaving us alone.

He looks at me. "Well, looks like you're here to take her place," he chuckles, trying to close the door, but it's pushed open with a bang.

I grin when I see Ryan strolling into the room like he owns it. "Now, what were you saying?" Ryan asks him and moves to stand slightly in front of me.

God, he looks so sexy right now. He is the ultimate alpha male. Power radiates off of him as he stares down this loser.

The loser looks at Ryan, his eyes wide. Of course all of his non-existent balls go straight out the window the second he stares down someone his own size.

"I have the wrong room, man. I'm supposed to be in the men's dorm." He tries to back out of the room like it was an accident.

Ryan reaches out, grabbing his arm before he can run off. "Nice fucking try. We need to talk." He pulls him out of the room, looking back at me and winking.

Why does he have to be so sexy? Since when do I have a thing for bad boys? Oh, I know when it was—the second I saw his arms flex when he was driving his bike. Then seeing how he is with my daughter, that just took the cake.

I move over to the bathroom door and knock. "He's gone, sweetheart."

A minute passes before Christa unlocks the door, her hand shaking as she gathers the nerve to come out.

"He is?" she asks to make sure.

"Yes, honey, he's gone and you will never see him again," I assure her. She lets out a deep breath and sits down on her bed. "Nobody said it would be easy leaving him, but anything is better than being beaten for just breathing," she whispers, addressing me but I have a feeling she's mostly saying it to herself.

I sit down beside her and hold her hand as long as she needs me. She tells me everything she has suffered in her life, that she wants to finish her schooling to be a nurse and that she wants kids someday.

A couple of hours later, there's a gentle knock on the door. I walk over and open it. I see Ryan first and I look down to see my precious angel standing next to him.

"Hi Momma!" Mia lifts her arms for me to take her and I pull her close, snuggling her. "I missed you so much today." I kiss her cheek and she giggles, twisting my name tag.

"Thank you for helping me today, Myra. I think I'm going to take a nap," Christa tells me, and I study her to make sure she's being truthful.

I relent. "Call me if you need anything, okay?" I tell her and leave my card on the desk by the door.

Ryan puts his hand on the small of my back, walking with me and Mia. "Ready to go home?" he asks.

Home. Is that what it is with him?

"Yeah I'm ready." He smiles back and takes Mia from me so I can get my bag. He walks in front of me and I can't resist the urge to tilt my head to the side, admiring his booty.

Oh yeah, I'm ready.

4

MYRA

LATER THAT NIGHT

RYAN WALKS into the room carrying his cellphone. "Get ready, I'm taking you out tonight. Chrystal and Kyle are going to come over to watch Mia for us," he says, completely out of the blue, and he leaves the room before I can even make a peep.

I look at the door he walked out of, floored that he just threw it out there like I'm going to agree just like that.

"Ryan is crazy, baby," I tell Mia, who just grins at me like she knows exactly what I'm talking about.

I sit down on the bar stool watching Mia play with her dolls. She loves brushing their hair over and over, so half of them are missing their hair because she's brushed them so much.

Ryan sticks his head in the doorway, smiling. "We're leaving in an hour. Wear jeans." He leaves once more.

I grumble to myself as I slide off the stool and do as he tells me to. I may be pretending that it's a hardship, but I really want some one-on-one time with Ryan.

Especially since we kissed. I can't help but think about it and what it could mean.

So I get dressed in my best jeans that make my butt look phenomenal and a black V-neck shirt, tucked in. I curl my hair slightly at the end to give it some volume and apply some natural eyeshadow and mascara.

Mia has been playing in the floor as I get ready. She really is the sweetest little angel. She rarely has temper tantrums or does anything she really shouldn't, but I probably just jinxed myself.

The hour passes fast. I walk into the living room with Mia. Chrystal is sitting on the couch with Cassandra, who just turned a year old a few weeks ago. She is the spitting image of Chrystal.

"Hi guys." I smile and Mia shakes her hand, trying to lose my grip. I let her go and she runs straight for Cassandra. "Babyyyy!" she screams, raising her arms out to hold her.

Chrystal helps Mia onto the couch and helps her hold Cassandra, who stares at Mia directly into her face. I smile at the sweet image.

Mia pats Cassandra's little leg gently. "Go to sweep, whittle baby." She makes little hushing sounds that just make my heart ache at the absolute cuteness.

"I think I have baby fever again," Chrystal sighs, staring at the both of them. I can't even deny that I want more kids. It's gotten to the point I've considered getting a sperm donor.

"Ready?" Ryan asks, breaking the moment.

He takes my hand and helps me off of the couch. "Goodbye, angel." I lean down and kiss the top of Mia's head, but she pays me no mind.

Ryan goes to her next, running his hand down her hair. "Bye, baby girl," his deep voice rumbles.

I may die from all of this.

Ryan turns his focus to Kyle. "Watch her."

Kyle finishes the sentence before Ryan can finish, "With my life."

I love the brotherhood all of these men have. They are rough and dangerous men without a doubt, but they share such a deep bond and they love wholeheartedly.

Ryan tugs on my hand, leading me out of the house straight to his bike parked in front of his house. "You ever rode on a bike before?" he asks.

I shake my head. "No, always wanted to though."

He smirks like the idea of me having never been on a bike before makes him happy. "Never had a woman on the back of my bike either."

Well that makes me feel way good. I'm the only girl who has ever been on the back of his bike.

He throws his massive thigh over the bike and lifts a hand out for me to take to steady myself as I slide in behind him.

I can't help but admire him. His cut makes him so much hotter. He turns his hat around and looks back at me slightly. "Ready?" He smiles, showing his teeth.

I scoot closer to him and wrap my arms around his middle, "Yes, sir."

I feel him jolt at me calling him sir—maybe I don't want to play fair anymore. I scoot even closer and plaster myself against his back, loving feeling his heat against me.

He rides through town and everyone stops and stares at him as he drives past. Some people wave, some people glare, but Ryan doesn't give any of them a second look.

He stops outside a restaurant. It's one of the newer ones in town and I pass it every day going to work.

This really is a date-date. He takes my hand, helping me off of the bike, and he follows me.

"Is this place fine?"

I smile, looking up at him. "The place doesn't matter, the company does."

He smiles, looking down at the ground. I can tell my statement made him happy. He doesn't let go of my hand but intertwines our fingers together instead. I love that.

We walk inside and we're seated swiftly. I scoot across the booth and Ryan slides in beside me.

I like that he wants to be close to me. Since I moved in it's pretty much been torture because he walks around shirtless in a pair of sweats. It should be a crime, especially since I can't touch him.

Just as the waitress comes up, she looks out of the window behind me. Her eyes widen and then she takes off running.

What the fuck?

I look out of the window just as a black SUV pulls up next to the window where I'm seated. I see the vest on the passenger's chest as a huge-ass gun pops out of the window.

I lock eyes with the guy with a gun and he smiles. Oh fuck. Fear is lodged deep into my chest. It's so deep, piercing, I know in this second that this is the end of me. I grab Ryan's leg and pray.

"Fuck!" Ryan roars loudly, scaring me and multiple people in the restaurant. He wraps his arm around my middle, jerking me out of the seat with him and he runs with me just as bullets pierce everything behind me.

People are screaming, glass shattering, bullets hitting everything in their path behind us.

I can't breathe, I can't move, I'm paralyzed as Ryan carries me through the restaurant away from the armed man.

We reach the back of the building and Ryan opens a storage closet and pushes me inside. "Stay here. I'll be back." He closes the door before I can even tell him fuck no and he better not leave me.

But here I am, shoved in the pitch black room, surrounded by cleaning supplies, but the thing that's haunting me isn't the dark, it's the sound of people screaming, crying.

My stomach turns and I try not to puke. I sit down on the floor and cover my ears.

I can't allow the guilt or fear to overpower me. I can't allow those emotions to take over in this moment, not when it comes to life or death.

Ryan

My heart stopped in my chest when I saw the gun pointed at her through the window. I didn't think, I just had to get her out of here, especially since I saw the shooter was Satan's Rejects.

They've found her.

I make my way into one of the offices in the back where the MC should have cameras. This restaurant is one the MC just opened in town.

I look at the cameras and see that we're pretty much fucking surrounded. Fuck me.

I text Kyle and tell him that shit has hit the fan and we need backup. Now for my sake, but I won't allow Myra to get hurt.

I care about her. That shit is something I didn't want to admit, but the second I saw her come into a room full of dangerous men and face us all to protect her daughter, I knew she was meant to be in my life.

I see one of the Rejects walk in the front door. Fuck.

I take my gun out of the back of my jeans and step around the corner, staying close to Myra but out of sight so I don't draw attention to where I stashed her.

"Come on, fucker," I whisper under my breath, waiting for one of them to show up.

They're pathetic, attacking a woman in the middle of a restaurant and hurting god knows how many innocent bystanders in the process.

All because she was defending herself and her baby.

These men don't deserve to breathe.

Footsteps sound from around the corner and I prepare. His gun is pointed towards the ground and I wait until he steps slightly past me before I wrap my arms around his neck, choking him until he passes out.

I shove him in the kitchen under the counter, out of sight. I peer back to the closet where Myra is sitting in.

I hear banging on the door from the outside. Fuck. I run over to the closet and pull her out. "Come on," I urge and she runs with me.

I hear the sound of the door breaking down and push her against the wall. I put my finger against my lips, wanting her to be quiet as I listen for footsteps.

She's gripping the front of my shirt, her eyes wide with fear, her skin paling by the second.

I wrap my arm around her, pulling her to my chest, and she wraps herself around me as tightly as she can.

I peer out to see if anyone is coming. "Come on, I'm going to sneak us outside," I whisper. She takes ahold of my arm and we sneak along the wall, ignoring the rampage that seems to be going on out in front.

"Where is she!" a man yells, and then a gunshot goes off. Myra jumps in shock at the sound.

I turn the corner to walk out the door they just broke down when I come face to face with a Reject.

I push Myra behind me and lift my gun, aiming before he can think, and shoot him in the neck.

He takes a step back, dropping his gun and clutching his neck with both hands. "There's action at the back!" someone yells from the front of the building.

"Oh god, Ryan," Myra whisper-yells and I close my eyes. "Walk in front of me, angel," I tell her calmly.

Myra

Walk in front of me, angel. This repeats over and over in my head. What does he mean? I'm not leaving him, that's for damn sure!

"Walk your ass in front of me," he says again, his voice devoid of emotion. I hesitate then walk in front of him. I look back to see him standing with his back to me.

"Go on, sweet girl," he says without looking back at me. That's when I hear someone coming straight down the hall towards him.

I see three men come around the corner to face Ryan. They lock eyes with me and I sneak out the door even though it absolutely kills me to do so.

I spot the guy that Ryan shot on the ground. I reach down and take his gun. I will not hide in fear, I will not allow this to go on.

I walk back inside, determined not to be afraid anymore. Ryan is fighting all of them at once as they try to run past him to me.

Ryan punches one of them in the face and he falls to the ground instantly and doesn't move.

I take the safety off of the gun and point it at one of the men who is trying to sneak up on Ryan.

Ryan turns around at the last second, grabbing him by the back of his head and smashes his face into the wall.

Another one joins the fray. I take my shot and shoot him in the leg. He doesn't make it another foot, falling to the ground in agony.

Ryan turns around to look at me, his eyes lit with fury before someone sneaks past him and grabs my arm, pulling me hard to him.

I gasp in shock and pull hard, trying to dislodge him.

Ryan grabs the arm holding me, ripping his fingers loose freeing me from my captor and pulling me behind him.

My heart sounds so hard, I can feel it up to my ears. Ryan pulls him closer, gripping him by the back of his hair just before dragging the knife across his throat.

He throws the man down to the ground, and I watch in horror as the man's blood pools around him as he chokes.

Ryan moves in front of me, blocking my view, gripping my jaw. "Get your ass in here." I shake my head no. He huffs, annoyed, lifting me off the ground, and throws me right back in the closet I was in before. "Apparently I'm going to babysit your ass." He smirks, smacking my ass, pushing me gently inside before slamming the door shut in my face.

Ryan

She is going to be the death of me. She doesn't listen. If she would have listened to me, she would be outside and away from all of these stupid fuckers.

Right now I have three on the ground groaning in pain and I hear more of those idiots running around the building trying to find me.

"Where is she?" one more yells, running into the room, and I look at the patch on his vest. I laugh, knowing this is the stupid fucker that she shot.

"What's it to you?" I taunt.

He stops dead in his tracks, "You dare to insult me?" His nose flares with anger.

"Or what?" I demand, stepping closer. This is the person who put a gun to Mia, who wants to hurt the both of them.

He is not going to die today, or tomorrow for that matter. No, he is going to suffer. He is going to know pain unlike he has known before. He is an open threat to the MC, and let's not forget he's threatening what's mine.

"I will kill you," he says with the most conviction he can muster, which isn't shit.

I roll my eyes. "Like that's going to happen. I've been waiting for you." That's when I hear the bikes. My brothers are here.

His face changes as the realization hits him. He starts to run, but I grab him by the back of the cut, slamming his face down onto the ground.

"You won't be needing this anymore." I take my knife and slit his vest down the back, making sure to drag it along his skin, fucking loving seeing the blood pooling.

"Fuck off!" he screams, trying to get up. I dig my knife right above his spine, daring him to push again so I can slide my knife into his spine like butter.

He freezes and I laugh, relishing the sounds of my brothers entering the building and making this a fair fight, the sound of him meeting his demise.

"Oh please fight some more," I gloat, but he doesn't move an inch. A few minutes later Torch walks into the room with Butcher behind him holding his blades.

"Took you fuckers long enough." I stand up and Torch picks the piece of shit up off the ground. "This is the guy that broke into Myra's house," I point out.

"Oh I remember his picture." Torch grins and smacks him in the face. "Too bad you didn't mind your own business, wasn't it? You could have just had one bullet wound. Now you're going to die a slow, painful death and Daddy won't be helping you."

I smile because it's true. He is going to die and he's going to face the wrath of every member of the Devil Souls MC.

Myra is mine and he just committed the ultimate sin: he dared to hurt what is mine.

5

MYRA

I'm still in this damn closet. I can hear voices outside but I can't get out since Ryan got smart and locked me inside.

Good thing I'm not scared of small spaces or I would have been screwed, "Let me out!" I bang on the door when I hear laughter.

A second later the door is pitched open and I'm faced with Ryan. "Took you long enough!" I hiss and push my way out of the dark room. "I need to go check on the people out in the dining room. They may need my services."

He takes my hand and stops me from leaving. "I'll go with you." He walks with me through the restaurant...or what's left of it at this point.

"Thank you for saving my life, Ryan," I whisper once we're alone in the hallway. I'm thankful because if it wasn't for him, I don't know what would have happened to me.

He stops dead in his tracks and turns to look at me, his eyes filled with fire. He doesn't say a word but his eyes say it all.

His hands go to my face, just before he picks me up off of the ground and presses my back against the wall, kissing me hard.

Devouring me.

I kiss him back just as hard. His hands squeeze my ass and he grinds himself against me, letting me know exactly how he's feeling about me right now.

Death, mayhem and a million other things are happening all around us, but all of that is gone and it's just us in this moment.

We have tiptoed around each other, heated looks and small little touches in passing.

He stops kissing me, both of us breathing hard. "Mine," he tells me, his voice deeper than before he started kissing me.

I smile, my breathing coming out in pants. I cup the side of his face and love feeling his stubble under my hand, the way his strong body is holding me, one hand holding me under my ass, the other buried in my hair.

We have been staring at each other for at least a minute before I speak. "We should probably go check on everyone."

He sets me down onto the ground gently, taking my hand again and pulling me closer, and we walk into the main part of the restaurant.

Chaos greets us. People are sitting around at the tables as police are walking around asking everyone questions.

I look around trying to find someone who seems to be injured. I just see a few people with minor cuts, but that's really it.

"Is no one hurt?" I ask Ryan, shocked, and one of the officers look around to me. "Just a few with some cuts and scrapes from broken glass. Shocked me too. It seems whoever this was was too busy worrying about something else."

I suck in my lips and Ryan tightens his grip on my side. We both stay quiet, not letting on to the fact that *I* was the target.

We don't stay. We get on Ryan's bike and I notice we head straight for the clubhouse. Soon after, Torch and Butcher pull up and ride behind us.

I wave at both of them, smiling. I'm thankful for what they're doing. They're putting their life on the line for me.

Butcher doesn't move, staring straight into my soul without emotion. Torch just nods. I don't think I've ever heard Butcher speak once the few times I've been around him.

We pull up in front of the clubhouse and I see Kyle waiting at the front with Techy. Is Mia okay? Ryan turns off the bike. "Is Mia okay?" I ask Kyle.

"She's currently asleep with Cassandra on the couch," he reassures me, and I let out a deep breath. The relief is instant.

Ryan takes my hand, holding me steady as I slide off the bike, but he doesn't let me go far and pulls me straight into his side.

I can tell his protective instincts are still in hyperdrive.

Kyle's phone goes off and he turns his head to the side, listening to whoever is on the phone. His head snaps up, looking towards the road.

That's when I see the SUV from earlier stopping dead outside of the gate.

It all happens in slow motion. I yell out Ryan's name, my stomach burning with fear.

He covers my body with his, throwing us to the ground. He covers my head with his arms, and I jolt with every blast of the gun hitting everything around us. "Please god don't let anyone get hurt," I whisper over and over.

"Shh, baby, it's okay," Ryan whispers in my ear.

I don't say anything, but it's not going to be okay if someone gets killed because of me.

A sliver of light peeks through when Ryan shifts. I turn around slightly to see everyone returning fire and the SUV still sitting outside of the gates shooting at everyone.

"I need to fucking get her out of here!" Ryan yells and then tightens his grip when another round of bullet fire in our direction hits his bike, the pings radiating all around us as dust flies.

Ryan lifts his body slightly, bringing his arm around my

middle, and starts to army crawl, carrying me, which I didn't think was possible.

Another spray of bullets surrounds us and has him stopping, and right in front of me, a bullet strikes.

This is pure mayhem. Kyle and the guys are returning fire, but we're stuck and I don't like feeling helpless.

"It's okay, sweetheart," Ryan whispers in my ear again, trying to soothe my fears.

"Ryan, I don't want you hurt," I whisper back. I think it would kill me if something happened to him and it would be all my fault.

"Don't fucking worry about me, angel. Just try to stay calm. I will get you out of here."

I don't reply. He shifts around me and that's when I notice that we're close to Ryan's truck.

He starts army crawling with me again, dragging me with him. I ignore the pavement dragging my skin as he keeps on going right under the truck to the other side, facing away from the shooters.

The second we're through, he snatches me up off the ground before I can even react and lifts me onto the seat of the truck. A bullet strikes the window but it doesn't pierce it.

"Be back, honey."

He opens the back seat and puts on a bulletproof vest, then grabs an AK 47 and I watch in horror as he walks right out into the gun spray, shooting.

They stop shooting as Ryan stalks over, trying to hide from his bullets, and one by one I watch them drop.

Ryan stalks right up to the gate with Butcher on his heels. Along with Kyle, they rip the gate open, pointing their guns.

I clutch my throat, my hand shaking as I try to breathe and snap back to reality. It's like I'm having an out-of-body experience. I can't believe all of this is happening.

Ryan pulls the trigger once more, the sound deafening. I

turn around and look out the front. I've seen enough—all I can handle.

I know these men had to die, it's me or them, but as a doctor it's hard. I close my eyes and rub my temples, trying to distract myself from what's happening right outside this glass.

I truly don't understand why these people want to kill me so much. I know that I shot the President's son or whatever, but he broke into my house and was going to hurt my daughter.

I did what I had to.

I don't regret that for a second, but I wish all of this wasn't happening and I got to have that date with Ryan.

The door is snatched open and my eyes fly open in fear and shock, but I relax when I see it's Ryan.

"It's okay, baby. It's just me." He touches my face, checking me over. I can see the concern on his face and that's enough to cause the tears to fall.

I sit up and face plant into his chest, taking comfort in feeling safe. He wraps his arms around me tightly and just holds me as I let it all out.

"Your tears are killing me," he tells me, but I can't help it. I've held it in since the very beginning and I just can't anymore. I'm human.

He buries his hand in my hair, pressing my face into his chest, clinging to me just as much as I am him.

"I have you." He presses his lips to the top of my head and I nod. He does and he proved that over and over today.

I lean back, touching his face. "I know you do." I kiss him softly, pouring all my emotions into the kiss because right now I don't have the words. All I have is feelings that have me feeling like I'm going to burst.

He holds me, kissing me so tenderly and carefully, making me feel so safe. I kiss him once more, looking up at him.

He smiles, causing my already frazzled stomach to flip. "Even though we almost fucking died today, you're still so beautiful." He kisses my forehead. I let the feelings just wash all over me.

"You ready to go home?" He pushes my hair behind my ear.

Home. That is what Ryan is to me.

"Yeah."

He taps my hip and I scoot over to the passenger seat while he climbs in the driver's.

"What about all of this mess?" I ask, looking out into the parking lot, where bodies are currently being dragged up towards the doors.

"The prospects will handle it." He doesn't even look over at the mayhem; it doesn't even faze him.

∽

The second we walk through the door, Mia runs straight for the both of us. "Momma! Ry-Ry!" she screams, throwing her little arms in the air for us to get her. I snatch her when she jumps in the air.

"Hello, my beautiful baby." I smother her in kisses and she giggles. I laugh with her. She makes me so happy.

She turns to Ryan. "Ry-Ry, missed you." She wiggles her fingers for her to hold him and my poor heart feels like it's going to explode. He takes her and kisses the top of her head. "I missed you too, baby girl."

She grins, resting her head on his chest, twisting her small fingers in his shirt. He sways side to side with a look of pure contentment on his face.

I rub my hand down her back. It's around eight a clock—time for her snack and bath time.

There's a knock at the door and we peer out the door. Kyle is here for Chrystal and Cassandra.

I kind of forgot she was even here, "Thank you so much for babysitting." She gets off the couch, holding Cassandra.

"It was no problem. I'll do it any time you need it." She walks over, giving me a side hug. Kyle takes Cassandra and they wave goodbye as they walk out.

Ryan goes to the wall, locking everything down for the night. "What snack do you want, honey?" I bring Mia into the kitchen and open the refrigerator.

She puts her hand on her face like she's studying the contents and points to the diced apples I cut for her earlier. I grab her sippy cup of milk.

"Want me to go get her jammies and run her bath?" Ryan asks as he walks upstairs.

"That would be great, honey," I tell him, and I catch his smile at me calling him "honey" as he walks up the stairs.

I give my darling my full attention as she eats her food and babbles in her baby talk. I will always remember these little moments because she won't be little forever.

Once she's finished with her snack, I bring her upstairs, which takes way longer than needed since she demands to walk up the stairs herself.

Ryan

The bathroom door opens and Mia walks out in her pajamas with little sheep on them, with a hairbrush in her hand.

She walks up to me, holding out the brush for me. "Ry-Ry?" She wiggles it and I take it.

I sit down on her bed, pulling her in my lap, and brush her hair gently. She sings under her breath, a song that she's making up as she goes and I try not laugh. "Momma, pee, toilet." She giggles covering her mouth. "Momma tooted in toilet!" I can barely understand her but it's hilarious.

Once I finish with her hair, I put the brush on the counter. "Lie down, sweetheart." I pull back the blanket and she climbs in.

"Want me to read you a story?" I take her story book off of the counter and her face brightens.

I lay down beside her, my back propped up against the headboard, and she scoots closer, lying on my arm so she can look at the pictures.

Myra

I get out of the shower and walk into Mia's bedroom. She's fast asleep and Ryan is still reading to her.

The sight of them together makes me happy. I walk over and touch his arm. "She's asleep."

He slowly slides off the bed, trying not to wake her. I start to lay on the ground next to her bed, but he takes my hand. "You sleep with me tonight." He doesn't leave room for arguments.

He pulls me out of the room, turning on a small little nightlight for Mia in case she wakes up in the middle of the night.

"Are you sure it's a good idea?" I ask, unsure, but I'm also out-of-this-world nervous. Sleeping in the same bedroom with him? That sounds like a disaster in the making.

"This house is a fortress, angel." He turns back enough to wink at me. Well, that leaves me with no argument.

He pushes open his door and I swallow hard, nervous. I've only been with one guy in my life and that was Mia's dad. It's been years since I've had sex.

He walks over to his chest of drawers and pulls out a T-shirt. "Want to sleep in this?"

Maybe his full intention is to just sleep? I walk over and take the shirt from him. "Thank you." I almost run into the bathroom. I try not to look at the bed because that alone makes me nervous.

I know without a doubt I'd love nothing more than to fall asleep in his arms. That sounds like pure heaven, but the thought of sex and him finding me lacking scares me.

He is beautiful. I feel like I'm way below his league and the thought of me not being exactly what he thought makes my heart ache.

I slip off my shorts and T-shirt, putting on his shirt, and I close my eyes, breathing in his scent that is all over the shirt. It's intoxicating.

My eyes close as I gather all of my balls. I open the door and step out just as Ryan pulls his sweatpants up.

My eyes drift down to his V, his abs rippling. I don't know how long I've been staring at him but I know it's an uncomfortable amount of time.

"You going to get in bed or just stare?" I blush deeply and shuffle to the bed. I could die of embarrassment.

Ryan laughs and scoops me up in bed, pulling me to him. "You're so adorable when you're embarrassed." His face is right above mine.

His hand drifts up to my face, my breathing stalling, waiting to see what he does next. His thumb strokes my cheek so gently. "You're beautiful, truly. All of you."

He continues to shock me. I can see that he's sincere. "Ryan," I whisper.

He doesn't say anything back, and his eyes go to my lips. My hand slides into his hair, scratching his scalp slightly.

Is he going to kiss me?

He licks his lips and my stomach does flips in my stomach as he comes closer, barely kissing me.

I don't dare move and I close my eyes.

"Baby," he whispers, his lips gliding over mine slightly.

Goose bumps break out across my skin. "Yes," I whisper back, my voice cracking slightly, giving away that I'm affected.

"Let me love you, all of you."

My eyes open at that and his immediately stare deep into my soul. There is no doubt in my mind that I want this, that I want him.

I nod.

He kisses me fully, devouring my mouth. My fingers run up and down his back, loving the feel of his muscles under the skin.

He kisses me in a way that steals every breath from my lungs. His hand moves up, cupping my face, tilting it to the side and kissing his way down to my neck.

His lips are so soft, sucking just slightly with every little kiss. You expect a man like him to be rough and tough, but with me he is so gentle.

That turns me on ten times more.

He's showing me the sweeter side of him, one that I'm sure not many people get to see.

"Lift your arms," he demands, sitting up and holding the bottom of my shirt.

I sit up slightly and allow him to pull the shirt over my head, leaving me bare. I didn't put on a bra when I got out of the shower.

My nipples pucker at his gaze. He cups my breast before running his finger over the tip of my nipple.

"Beautiful."

He slides down the bed, kissing me once more before he runs his hand up and down my thigh.

His mouth is right above my breast, torturing me, teasing me. "Ryan," I whisper, dying. It's taking everything in me to cover myself.

I had a baby—some things don't go back to what it was before. I have stretch marks and cellulite all over my body.

He smiles right before his mouth closes around my nipple, sucking slightly before his tongue soothes it.

I throw my head back. I was not expecting that. I open my legs to fit him in between my legs better and I can't resist tilting my hips to feel his erection against me.

"Mmm, is my baby hungry?" Ryan grinds himself against me, moving to my other breast, sucking deep.

My hands fly up, burying into his hair, needing to hold on to something. "Let's see how much you need me." His hand slips into my panties, his fingers dancing across my clit.

"Drenched." He smirks. He slides down the bed, gripping my legs. "I bet you I can make you wetter."

His fist grips my panties, tearing them down my legs. He opens my legs, looking at me fully and licking his lips.

Oh god, no one has ever done this before.

I cover my face, waiting, but his hand tugs on my arm. "Look at me. I want you to see exactly how I worship you. Do not be ashamed, baby." He smiles softly right before he goes back to his smirk.

I watch as he oh-so slowly moves closer and closer, and I grow wetter by the second. It's torture waiting. He wants to make me want him.

He's destroyed me and he's barely touched me.

Finally, he looks me straight in the eye as he licks me fully. I grip the covers under me. "Fuck," I groan, and he chuckles, swirling his tongue over my clit before flicking the tip.

His hands scoot under me, gripping my ass. He lifts me higher off the bed so he can have better access.

"This pussy is mine," he growls before he eats me like a man possessed, letting me know that he owns all of me.

I can't move, I can't breathe as the orgasm draws closer and closer, the pleasure almost too much to handle, but I want more and more.

My legs shake, sweat covering me from head to toe. I long forgot to look at Ryan as the pleasure is the only thing I can think about.

He slips two fingers inside of me and I stop breathing as he curls his fingers, sending me over the edge, clenching over and over around his fingers.

I feel movement on the bed when he climbs off. I stare at him as he slips off his clothes, leaving him naked.

I have never seen anything so beautiful in my life.

Then I look down at his dick and my mouth dries because he's not going to fit.

"What's that scared look on your face, sweet thang?" he chuckles and grabs a condom out of the nightstand next to the bed.

I point to his dick resting against his belly. He looks down and smirks, then reaches between my legs, grabbing my wetness. He strokes his dick, his face full of passion.

You know, I don't care if I die. What a flipping amazing way to go.

"I'll fit, baby, you were made for me." His voice grows huskier.

My heart swells at his sweet statement. I open my arms as he moves on top of me. My arms wrap around his neck, holding him tightly as I kiss him.

I feel him move between my legs, his fingers stroking my clit when his head presses against my entrance.

I relax, trusting him to take care of me. He presses his way inside so gently, taking such care to not hurt me.

I wrap my legs around his waist. He stops kissing me to look into my eyes and he slowly makes his way inside.

I don't feel any pain, just slight burning as my body gets adjusted to him. "You okay?"

I run my nails slightly down his back. "I'm more than okay." I lean up, kissing him again as he pulls all the way out before slamming back inside.

"God." I break the kiss, throwing my head back. My pussy immediately tightens around him at the intense pleasure

Ryan grips my thigh, lifting my leg higher, and that's when he really starts to move, grinding into my clit with every slam.

His hand comes up, cupping my neck, his eyes burrowing deep into mine. "You are mine—all of you belongs to me." His hand flexes against my neck before he kisses me hard and my nails rake up his back.

His hand sneaks in between our bodies, his thumb rubbing my clit. I throw my face into his neck and come hard, my whole body shaking. My legs slide off his back and onto the bed.

He comes right along with me, moaning in my ear and gripping me hard, holding me tightly against him.

Slowly we collect our bearings, sitting in silence for the last five minutes, and in my head I'm thinking, *holy shit I just had sex with Ryan and he was just as good as he looks.*

And he looks fucking great.

When he slowly slides out of me, I can barely hide the wince. He struts into the bathroom and my eyes are glued to the fantastic ass he has.

I hear the water running in the bathroom and I'm too tired to get up. He comes out of the bathroom carrying a washcloth.

"What are you doing?" I ask once he stands next to me. He grabs my legs, opening them, and uses the washcloth to clean me.

If I didn't already love this man, that would have done it. Tears pool in my eyes for many reason, but mostly my heart is absolutely full.

Ryan looks up and notices. He swipes his finger across my cheek. "Did I hurt you?" he asks, and now I feel awful for making him think that.

"No, I'm just happy," I confess, and I *am* happy, wholeheartedly happy.

He leans down and kisses me so sweetly on the forehead. "You make me happy too, baby. You have the second you walked into my life, and Mia completed that life."

Wow, just wow.

I reach up and pull him into bed with me, just needing to hold him and him to hold me.

He pulls my face into his chest, his hand resting on the back of my head protectively.

Why do I have a feeling that this is where I'm going to spend the rest of my life?

Myra

"Mama." My eyes shoot open instantly, then I hear the sound I know all too well—my daughter puking all over the floor.

I jump out of bed, and before I can reach her, Ryan picks her up, carrying her to the bathroom.

She is crying hysterically. I rub her little belly and back, trying to soothe her. She continues to puke and puke.

"Come on, sweet girl. Let's give you a bath. I turn on the water and strip her out of her nasty pajamas. She clings to me, shaking and scared, and reaches out to hold Ryan's hand.

"I'll be right back, angel. I'm going to get you some new pajamas and clean up the puke." He starts to stand and she screams, holding tighter to his hand.

I see the anguish on his face. "I won't leave you, angel." He takes her from me and sets her in the tub. I think she has the same feeling as I do.

He makes her feel safe when she's scared and not feeling well. He sits right on the floor with me as I bathe her as fast as possible in case she gets sick again.

Ryan wraps her in a towel, lifting her out and holding her close to his chest so sweetly. "Ry-Ry," she whispers, and my heart melts at the pure look of love on his face. He loves my girl.

He lays his head on top of hers, carrying her out into the bedroom and my eyes go to the huge spot of vomit.

"I'll grab her pajamas." I run to her bedroom and grab a few extras just in case then hurry back.

Ryan is rocking her side to side, half asleep. I hand him the clothes and he takes them from me, gently getting her dressed, and I hurry to clean before it stinks up the room.

"Want her to sleep with us?" Ryan asks and covers her with the blanket, her head lying on his leg.

"Yeah, it's probably best. I'm going to get her some Pedialyte. I don't want her to get dehydrated." Ryan starts to get up and she clings to him like a monkey, crawling back up him until he's holding her.

He looks guilty. "It's okay," I mouth, and he rubs her back, trying to get her to calm down. He nods and pulls the blanket up, covering her back. I can see her shaking.

Ryan

I FEEL LIKE A DICK BECAUSE MYRA IS CLEANING UP EVERYTHING but I can't tell Mia no. She is fast asleep against my chest and if I move just slightly, she wakes up scared.

Myra comes back in the room. She's beautiful. Her hair is a mess, but knowing I did that makes me damn happy.

"Sweetheart, you need to drink this." Myra hands her the sippy cup and Mia looks at me like she wants me to feed her.

I smile and take it, feeding her like she's a small baby. I don't mind it. I love that she wants me around her for comfort right now.

I worry about shit a lot when it comes to Mia. I'm afraid I'm not going to do everything right and fuck her up somehow, but right now I think she truly likes me.

I look at Myra and Mia and I see my right now and my future,. I can see Myra carrying our babies one day and Mia being a big sister.

I saw that shit the second she walked into the room at the clubhouse pleading her case.

I knew then and right now I'm even more sure.

I wrap my free hand around the back of Myra's head and pull her to me, kissing her. She smiles and rests her face against my neck.

Life is pretty fucking perfect.

6

RYAN

ONE WEEK LATER

Today is the day I hope to end all of this shit with the Satan's Rejects. We have a meeting with the President.

We're meeting outside of our town in the middle of nowhere, because if shit goes bad then there won't be any witnesses.

I want Myra and Mia to have a normal fucking life. It's wearing on her more and more every day. The last straw was yesterday when a vehicle backfired and she panicked. I've never seen her that scared, even when she was shot at.

We hear the bikes before we see them and we stand, waiting. Butcher is behind us, pacing, ready for murder.

They pull up in front of us, trying to make a show by revving up their engines, and I resist the urge to roll my eyes.

These bikers are fucking pathetic. They would be lucky if we even allowed them to leave here alive.

I don't take too fucking kindly to those I care about being threatened and neither do my brothers.

The President, named Diablo, gets off his bike, walking over to face us, and his members all pool around him.

It's taking everything in my power to not just reach over and strangle him. It sickens every part of me to be in front of him.

"What's the meaning of this?"

"What will it take to end your feud with Myra?" Kyle speaks up, stepping out slightly in front of us to show that he is our President.

Diablo looks at Kyle and then the rest of us. "One hundred thousand."

I don't even bother to stifle the laugh that escapes me. His eyes narrow on me and his guys reach for their guns.

"Something funny?" he asks.

I smirk, stepping out and standing next to Kyle. "You are fucking delusional if you think I'm going to pay you a dime. How about you end this shit before I end your fucking life, hmm?"

My brothers gather at my back, backing my words. I grin because I see the slight fear in his eyes. I arch an eyebrow, letting him know exactly that I know.

He looks from me to Kyle. "Where's my son?"

"Dead," Kyle deadpans, and we all laugh because all of the Rejects take a step back. Finally they realize that we're not fucking around.

We are not the type to play games. We end them.

"You killed him?"

"Yeah we did. He showed up our gate and was trying to shoot *my* woman, *my* ole lady. That shit comes with repercussions. So your choice is to die or accept the offer because I will offer that only once." I get right in his face, loving every second of him flinching with every word.

He looks away from me to the ground before he looks at Kyle. "We accept."

They don't even deserve the title of MC—they are straight pussies. I would have slit someone's throat if they came to me with these demands, but we are not them. We have honor.

"But as a small price for your sins against us, we will take your trigger finger as payment for the bullets you tried to shed against one of ours." Kyle tells him the final demand.

Diablo's face pales. "Or die, your choice," Kyle finishes, taking out his knife and running his hand along the tip.

Kyle hands me the knife and I take it, waiting for Diablo to man up.

He steps toward me and I grip his hand before he can back away. He tries to pull away. I glare at him hard, daring him to move.

He turns his head away and I run the knife over his finger over and over, loving every second of his screams.

Call me sick but I savor that shit. It's a small price for what Myra has suffered. I throw the finger onto the ground and they all run off, getting on their bikes, like dogs with their tails between their legs.

"Ready to go home?" Kyle asks, and we all load up, watching the bikes drive away.

~

Myra

I'M NOT GOING TO LIE AND PRETEND THAT I DIDN'T STAY UP TO wait on Ryan to get home, I saw him leave with his bulletproof vest.

I have my phone in my hand in case one of them got hurt and they needed me. Mia is asleep in her bedroom. The both of us got her to sleep before he left.

The second I saw him leave out the door, I watched him change before my very eyes. I saw Ryan the Devil Souls MC member come out.

I see him pull into the yard and I want to sink to the ground with relief, but I turn on the TV to pretend that I didn't just sit here in silence with worry filling my heart.

He walks through the door and throws his keys on the table by the door. "Hi honey," I say softly. I love to see him softening for me.

There are so many layers to Ryan. I reach out my hand for him to take and I pull him onto the couch with me.

"You okay?" I can't resist the urge to ask and not check him from head to toe to make sure of it.

He kisses my temple. "Everything is fine, angel, but there is something I need to tell you."

Oh no. My stomach sinks and I look at him. I know I have fear written all over my face.

"Yes?"

He takes my hand, running his thumb across the top. "We met with the President of the Satan's Rejects tonight. We came to an agreement. It's all over, sweetheart."

The world is lifted off of my shoulders and I want to weep with joy, but the other part of me is terrified because this means that I have no reason to be here anymore.

His expression changes to one of confusion and he cups my face. "Why the long face?"

"So I leave now?"

He jumps like I shocked him. "What are you talking about?"

I pull my hands from his. "We have no reason to be here anymore. You don't need to protect us." Sadness is filling my heart by the second. I can't even imagine how Mia will react to him not being in her life, nor mine.

Ryan slides off the couch and moves in front of me on his knees, "That is the dumbest shit I have ever heard in my life." He stops, taking a deep breath.

"Sweetheart." He takes my hand and presses it against his heart. "This belongs to you, you and that precious baby asleep upstairs. I will always protect you, now and until I die. I don't want you to leave. I want you to spend the rest of your life with me. I want you to be my ole lady, my life and the mother of our kids."

I'm speechless. I never expected him to tell me that. "I love you, Ryan. My whole heart and my entire being belongs to you." I press my lips to him, pouring every feeling into that kiss.

This second moment changed our whole entire life—we have found our forever.

Me and Mia are finally…

Home.

EPILOGUE

MIA

Eighteen Years Old

I GREW up watching my dad and mom have the kind of love that belongs in fairy tales, the kind of love you can only dream about.

Each day they showed us how much they loved and supported us, me and my brothers.

Dad protected us, sheltered us and built us to be this unstoppable force to take no shit from anyone and to never apologize for being ourselves.

Mom nurtured us, healed every ache and pain we had in life and taught us how to be kind and love fully.

They gave us a life that I will forever cherish and the life I should strive for.

I smile when I hear the small little pebbles clicking against my window. I lock the door and throw open my window, looking down at my secret boyfriend.

Ashton.

Ashton is someone my dad wouldn't approve of. You know why?

Because Ashton happens to be the son of the President of a rival MC.

"Come down, sweetheart, let's go for a ride," he says in that sexy voice of his.

God, I am in such trouble.

Printed in Great Britain
by Amazon